To Pr

Under Your Skin

Rose McClelland

Love, Rose xx

DARK
STROKE

www.darkstroke.com

Discover us online:
www.darkstroke.com

Find us on instagram:
www.instagram.com/darkstrokebooks

Include **#darkstroke** in a photo of yourself
holding this book on Instagram and
something nice will happen.

In memory of Snowy McClelland
29 December 2016 – 6 January 2020

About the Author

'Under Your Skin' is Rose's fourth novel. Her previous three were romantic fiction published by Crooked Cat. She has made the genre jump from 'chick lit' to psychological thriller and is enjoying delving into a darker corner of her mind!

Rose has also written two short plays which were performed in the Black Box theatre in Belfast.
She discusses book reviews on her You Tube channel and writes theatre reviews for her blog.

She loves nothing more than curling up with her cats and a good book. She has two rescue cats – Toots, who is ginger with an inquisitive face and Soots, who is black and hops along on his three legs looking ever so cute.

Acknowledgements

Thank you to my sister Rhoda for painstakingly reading every single chapter of draft one and giving me feedback as I went. Thank you also for the gentle reminder emails, "What about the next chapter? Have you written it yet?"

Thanks to Debbie and Ruth for their support and constant sharing of book news on social media.
Thanks to Joe and Ann for continued emotional support.

Thanks to Laurence and Steph of darkstroke for believing in me and my book. Thanks Laurence for the wonderful editing skills and for moulding this manuscript into shape!

Thanks to you the reader for buying this book. I hope you enjoy reading it as much as I enjoyed writing it.

Under Your Skin

Chapter One

Kyle

"999, what's your emergency?"

"It's my wife," Kyle blurts out. "She's gone missing."

"How long has she been missing?" the calm, monotone responder asks.

"It's been since nine this morning," he says, impatience lacing his every word.

"So that's…" Calm voice must be counting on her fingers. "Twelve hours?"

"Yes," he bites back. "I guess. Yes, twelve hours. It's not like her. She's always home by now."

Miss Calm asks, "Any history of mental illness, sir?"

He blanches. "Who? Me?"

"No sir. Your wife?"

He bites his lip. "No," he begins. "No, I guess not." Although there was that time the doctor suggested antidepressants. But no matter. Miss Calm is now on to the next question.

"So tell me what happened. When was the last time you saw her? What mood was she in? Had there been any arguments?"

Arguments? Well yes, there had been, but that was hardly relevant.

"I saw her this morning before she headed to work. She was fine. I came home at eight tonight and she's not here. She's not answering her mobile. It's not like her. I'm convinced something has happened. What if some rapist has captured her? The sooner the police look for her, the better!"

He realises that his voice is rising in octave with each

sentence, but he can't help it. What's the point in talking so slowly on the phone when she could be sending a cop out straight away to look for her!

He feels his breathing quicken and walks over to the counter to pick up his packet of cigarettes. He pulls one out of the packet and tinges the end with his lighter.

"Can I take your name sir?" the responder asks, her voice too slow for Kyle's liking.

"Kyle Greer," he rattles off impatiently.

"And your wife's name?"

"Hannah. Hannah Greer. Please hurry."

But the responder maintains her calm, professional, monotone voice. "And your address?"

"One one seven Raven Reach, Belfast," Kyle spits out each word as though his quick-fire responses might hasten the arrival of a policeman.

"Okay Mister Greer," the calm responder answers with a heavy sigh. "We've put that on record. But I'd suggest you phone us back tomorrow if there's still no sign of her. She may well return this evening."

Kyle's eyes widen. "So nothing's going to be done?"

"We usually wait at least twenty-four hours sir, in the case of an able-bodied adult. Of course, if it was a child or a vulnerable elderly then…"

"Fine," Kyle cuts in. "I'll phone back tomorrow. Thanks for your help," he spits, with a large dose of sarcasm. He clicks the off button and heads towards the kitchen. With his cigarette dangling in the side of his mouth, he pours himself a large glass of Vodka and Coke. Noticing that his hands are shaking, probably with anger at how unhelpful the responder had been, he gulps back the drink greedily. He re-fills his glass for good measure, walks towards the back door and sits on the back doorstep, smoking the rest of his cigarette and knocking back the drink. The night air is quiet; too quiet. He sits and waits. And while he's waiting, he can feel the warmth of the drink start to trickle down to his toes.

Chapter Two

<u>Hannah</u>

I'm in a basement. If I crane my neck enough and reach up on the worktop, I can peer out the small window at the top. I can see people coming and going, their shoes walking past. Smart business shoes in the morning; high-heeled shoes in the evening. An assortment of trainers and workmen boots throughout the day.

I wonder if Kyle has phoned the police. I wonder if a 'missing person' campaign has been launched. I could almost picture it. Would they run a Facebook campaign? Would they organise a "Hashtag Hannah" on Twitter? I wonder if they'd organise a group of people to walk up Cavehill, searching behind every hedgerow for me. That didn't seem right. All those poor people scaling the heights of Belfast in wet and windy weather, while I'm tucked all the way down here in this basement. There's absolutely no way anyone would find me. Even if I tried to batter on the tiny window at people's feet, no-one would hear. The window is too thick, so I couldn't break it. No-one would hear anything over the noise of the traffic.

The one saving grace is that he's given me drugs. That's the only thing I said to him. "Please, above everything, can you please just get me my tablets?"

I don't think he cared; don't think he minded. As long as it calmed me down, kept me quiet, shut me up. As long as I didn't make any fuss. He'd unlock the door, a hand would poke through, and a box would be set on the floor. Then he'd lock the door again and he was away.

I'd scramble over to the box like a child desperate to open her Christmas presents. I'd tear open the box and the foil packaging would tumble out. Lots of lovely tablets all encased in silver foil.

"Hello," I'd say, in a soft purr, as though I was greeting a lover. "Come to me."

I'd pop the pills out of the packaging. Plop, plop, plop. One after the other. Like Smarties out of a cylinder tube.

I'd set them on my tongue and gulp back some lukewarm water, letting the tablets travel down to my stomach, on their way to digestion. Soon I'd be feeling their effects. The warmth. The wooziness. The feeling like I've been wrapped in cotton wool. And then I wouldn't care. Wouldn't care about anything. Wouldn't care about the basement. Or being tucked away. Wouldn't care about Kyle. Wouldn't care about a likely police search. I'd just be drifting. On my own soft cotton wool cloud, encased in a metaphorical duvet, sleeping the night away.

Chapter Three

Kerry

"Kerry, have you got an hour? I need you to come out on a missing persons."

I gulp and look up to see DCI Simon calling over at me as he charges into the office.

"Uh... sure," I agree, jumping to my feet and pulling my jacket from behind my chair. My still un-drunk mug of coffee sits longingly on my desk and I can't resist leaning over to take one last grateful gulp.

"Great," he replies, pulling his own jacket from the stand and walking out of the office, expecting me to follow suit. "It's in East Belfast; upper end of Ravenhill Road." He talks as he walks, briefing me on the job en route to save time. "Woman went missing two days ago. Hannah Greer. Thirty-two years old. Married to Kyle Greer. It was Kyle who made the call."

I follow him down the flight of stairs and out into the foyer. I try to ignore the raised glances from the receptionist and other junior female officers. No doubt they'd be jealous that I'm getting to hang out with "Scrummy Simon" (as he's secretly known behind his back). Scrummy Simon is the eye candy for all the females at Musgrave Police Station. With his good looks and fit physique, he could pass for any high street model. But not only that, he has a decent personality too – chatty, charismatic, friendly. Most of the female officers swoon at how lucky his wife is. Simon is the full package.

"We'll take my car," Simon says as he strolls over to his silver Audi. Winking at me he adds, "Wouldn't look good for my image to be seen in your yellow Beetle."

I feign mock surprise and pretend to talk to my bright yellow vehicle which is parked near his flashy number. "Don't listen to him Daisy. You're the perfect car."

I don't know how Simon brings out the playful banter side in me. Normally I'd be way too intimidated to banter with the higher echelons of the Police force – never mind so obviously a gorgeous one – but perhaps it's because he's a married man. He has that immediate off-limits vibe which means it doesn't really matter. It's not as if I'm trying to impress him.

Starting up his car and driving us out of the high security barriers, Simon continues with his briefing. "Turns out Kyle phoned the minute he returned home from work and found that Hannah wasn't there. Sounds like she's the type tied to the kitchen sink."

I frown. "What? So she's not even allowed a quick drink with the girls after work?"

Simon shakes his head. "Seems not."

"Sounds like your wife Laura," I jibe playfully.

Simon throws me a mock scornful look. "Quite the opposite. Laura's never in. Never know where she is half the time."

I'm tempted to probe but think that would be crossing the line just a tad. Playful banter is one thing. Being nosey with the boss is quite another.

When we pull up outside the house, I'm struck by how pretty it looks. Autumnal leaves are scattered all around the front path, making it look like something out of a picture postcard. The front door is bright red and the entire building is in a rustic red brick. It looks like a proper three storey family home, one I'd love to see myself living in one day, complete with husband and two kids. Alas, it doesn't look like things are going to go that way for me. But I push that thought aside. Now is not the time to be morose and speculative. Now is the time to be professional. I notice the familiar surge of adrenaline rise as we reach the red door and tap loudly on the brass knocker.

Within minutes a well-dressed man arrives at the door.

"Kyle Greer?" Simon asks.

Kyle nods.

"Detective Inspector Simon Peters," Simon says, holding up his badge.

"And I'm Kerry Lawlor," I add, holding up my own police ID.

"Come in," Kyle says immediately. He is polite and formal, but I can see the pain and worry etched on his face.

Leading us into the hallway, I'm in awe of how beautiful and modern the house is. A large winding staircase. Wooden floorboards. Pretty furniture displaying cosy candles and figurines. Mirrors along the walls give the impression of an even larger space. My first thought is: money. Is this a financially driven case? Is she being held ransom in return for a financial pay-out?

Kyle leads us into the front room. The same grandiosity continues. There are two large plush sofas in 'L' shapes, a huge TV on the wall, plants and a piano. The room gives the air of money but not of children. There are no toys lying around, no sign of any messiness or playfulness. Everything is in its place.

"Do you have any kids?" Simon asks, mirroring my thoughts.

Kyle shakes his head no. His face hides something – annoyance at being asked this question? Regret that they don't have kids? Inability to have them?

"Did you ever want kids?" Simon asks. I notice Kyle bristling. Clearly this is a touchy subject.

"Mr Greer," I interject softly. "If it appears that we're asking a lot of intrusive questions, please forgive us. We're only trying to paint as full a picture as possible in order to help you find your wife."

I immediately see Kyle's shoulders relax a little.

"You're right," he says. "Sorry." Then he indicates towards the sofas. "Please sit."

We sit on the plush sofas and I try to sit upright and appear professional even though the sofa begs me to sink into it and relax.

"Do you want a coffee or anything?" Kyle asks.

"No thanks, we're fine." Simon answers for us. "We don't want to take up too much of your time."

Speak for yourself, I think. *I could murder a coffee.*

"So," Simon continues, "Let's retrace the steps. Tell us about the last time you saw Hannah. What form was she in? How was her mental state?"

Kyle looks irritated by that question. "Why does everyone keep asking about her mental state? She was fine! It was just a normal day, she was heading to work like any other day."

"I see," Simon says, his fingers resting on his chin. "And no history of depression?"

I interject again. "Er, it's quite common, Mr Greer, that missing persons are suffering depressive thoughts or suicidal tendencies... it's not always the case of course but..."

"She was fine," Kyle states again, with a slightly abrupt tone to his voice. "She had no reason to disappear, which makes me think that someone has captured her... a rapist or something..." he trails off as though the thought of it is too distressing.

"Do you know what?" I say. "I'd love a coffee after all actually. Shall I make it? I'm happy to help myself?"

Chapter Four

Hannah

It's like a prison, being in here. This is what it must be like for prisoners. All this time, just to sit and think. Time flies, people say, when they've had a fantastic summer and the weeks and months have flown by effortlessly.

Time flies, people say, when they realise that their beloved children have already whizzed all the way through Primary School and Secondary School and now they're considering what Uni to attend.

Time flies when it's a Friday afternoon and the mood is good and everyone's in high spirits looking forward to the upcoming weekend with all its festivities and relaxation time.

Time drags when it's a Monday morning and a foggy hangover has not yet lifted. When the thought of a long week looms ahead.

Time drags when you're sitting in the dentist waiting room listening to the drill of the poor unfortunate ahead of you, knowing that you're next.

Time drags when you're in a basement, locked away from the outside world, not knowing how long you'll be there for or what's going to happen next.

In a way, I didn't mind the thinking time. The introversion. The isolation. I had always been a bit of an introvert, preferring to have my head stuck in a good book rather than be the centre of attention at a social gathering. Mum used to take us to the library as kids and I'd have my four allotted books devoured in no time.

I don't have any books here. I make a mental note to ask him for books the next time he comes down. Books and drugs. As long I have those, I'll survive. The drugs give me that cotton wool feeling that protects me from everything – makes me not give a shit. And the books help me to escape into another world. They take me out of my head and into someone else's life; someone whose life is far from living in a basement.

I idly wonder about Kyle. I think about what he's doing now. I imagine he'll be on the phone to the police, reporting my disappearance. I imagine a Facebook campaign; my picture on posters around town, plastered on pub doors and corner shop windows. I imagine the pressure the police would be under as they try to find me. I pity them in a way. All those stresses and strains of everyday life. Whereas here's me, introverting in this cocoon, quietly off my face, not having to do anything except sit here and wait. Like a really bad game of hide and seek.

I think back to when Kyle and I first met. That's what happens when you have lots of time on your hands. You start reminiscing about your past. I wonder if this is what they mean when they say about your life flashing across your eyes.

***

I was so wow'ed by Kyle. The way he sauntered in and plopped himself on the edge of my desk.

"So, you're new here?" he'd asked.

He was gorgeous. Black hair, lovely features, slim build, and a charm and charisma that was irresistible.

"Yes," I murmured, nervously. "I'm Hannah."

"Kyle," he said, in response. "Hope you like it here. We're not a bad bunch, I swear."

I laughed nervously. Damn! Why couldn't I think up some interesting repartee? Why did I have to giggle like a silly teenager?

"We all go for drinks after work on a Friday. You should come," he said lightly, and then he was gone. Just like that.

Well, how could I just turn up for drinks? What pub did

they go to? Would I be going along with him? Or would I need to find some female colleague to latch on to?

The irrationality and unsteadiness of his invite both excited and irritated me in equal measures. Why didn't he just ask me out properly instead of being so casual?

Still, it wouldn't be a good idea to date someone at work. And besides, I certainly didn't have the nerve to turn up on my own and latch on to him, in the hope that his invite was more personal than just a group free-for-all. I put the thought out of my head and didn't bother going. I went home instead and ordered some takeaway and wondered how their night was going. I wondered about the girls he'd be chatting up; what girl he'd be taking home; what the gossip would be next week. With a heavy heart I took myself off to bed, resigning to the fact that he was way out of my league anyway.

"You didn't come for drinks," he stated the following Monday.

"No… I …," I faltered.

"Why not?" he persisted.

"I didn't know where it was… I …," I trailed off.

"All Bar One, on the High Street," he answered, his clear and confident voice showing absolutely no nerves. "Meet me in the foyer at five on Friday – walk round with me."

I nodded slowly, "Okay…," I replied, trying to hide my nerves and excitement.

I did meet in the foyer. He was running a little bit late and I was about to give up and head home, chiding myself for really believing that this faux 'date' was happening. But then I saw him, running down the stairs and throwing a cheeky grin in my direction.

"Sorry I'm a bit late," he piped up. "That old bugger would chain me to the desk all weekend if he could."

I wanted to flirt so badly. I wanted to make some comment about how I wouldn't mind chaining him to the desk either, but of course it didn't materialise. Instead a simple, "Aww, that's okay, don't worry," came out.

He laced his hand through my arm and walked me in the direction of the pub. Honestly, my legs really did feel like jelly. People say that like it's just some well-worn cliché, but that's the physical reaction I had.

Thankfully he did all the talking because I was far too nervous to come up with any clever repartee. I think I knew that this night was a big deal, and I knew I'd always look back on it. He chatted away about work and how busy his day had been, and I listened and made all the appreciative noises in the right places. And then we arrived in the pub.

It hit me the moment I entered. The smell of alcohol, the smell of fun, of freedom, of letting your hair down for one night only. Kyle bought me a glass of wine and we found a booth to sit in. Some other work colleagues came over to join us and I was grateful that I could sink into the background, letting the others do the talking whilst I smiled and laughed at their stories.

After three glasses on an empty stomach, all my nerves had evaporated. It helped that he was so talkative, asking me open questions, listening and then chatting away with his own responses. Gradually my humorous side came out, and maybe even a little bit of flirtation did too. He smiled at me appreciatively, as if he was waiting for this, as if he knew all along that underneath the shyness was a fun-loving girl.

But it was more than that. I felt something. It was almost tangible. A magnetic force. A chemistry. An invisible elastic band that drew us together. I could feel that I was falling in love with him. I could see it right in front of my very eyes.

At the end of the night he led me outside and said something about making sure I got into a taxi. But in the cool night air, away from the stares of our colleagues, he stood close to me and looked down at me with those sincere, charming brown eyes.

"I've had a great time with you tonight Hannah," he said softly.

"Mm, me too," I agreed, the alcohol making me loose and free.

His hands rested on my elbows and I could feel him pressing himself closer to me.

"I'd really like to see you again soon," he said.

I looked up and him and smiled, our mouths now tantalisingly close. "I'd like that too."

And then he was kissing me, soft, slow kisses at first, and then kisses that became harder and more passionate.

Suddenly he broke off from me. "Shit, I better stop," he said. "I'm getting too carried away."

I giggled. "It's okay. I was enjoying it."

I kind of expected him to come back to my place. I kind of wanted one night of rampant sex and then for us to ignore each other in work forever more. But it didn't happen like that.

He didn't ask to share a taxi. He made sure that I got in a taxi, and then he gave me one last peck on the lips and said, "I'll call you."

And that was that. The taxi drove off and he was standing there waving, and I thought, *How? How will you call me? You don't have my number.*

But he must have got it from one of my colleagues because the next day he texted me and invited me out for food. And that was the start of it. Candlelit dinners, nights out to the theatre, nights-in cooking a lovely meal and sharing a bottle of wine; those early weeks of blossoming romance. He sent me songs that were so beautiful and mesmerising that they sank down to the very recesses of my heart and melted there. Something changed in me. I felt different. Like the world had opened up like a delicate flower and everything looked beautiful. The sky looked bluer. Birdsong sounded more beautiful. The clouds appeared more white and fluffy. As if a filter had been added to the world giving it an extra rose-tinted glow.

He bought me presents – boxes of chocolates and bunches of flowers and pretty notebooks. It was one of those times when I was being wooed and romanced and I look back at that time and I think 'Stop!' Why didn't I stop and appreciate every moment? Because when you're in a moment like that, you assume that it will last forever – but it doesn't. It's fleeting and fast. Here one day and gone the next. One day you're being romanced and thinking it'll last forever and the next you're in a basement seeing your life flash before your eyes.

***

I take four more tablets and wash them down with water. Then I take another two for good measure. Soon the wooziness will kick in and I distract myself with more good memories. I remember the time he first told me he loved me. It was very early on – after only a few weeks. He sent me an email. Hidden in lines and lines of asterisks, was

******I********L**o**v**e*******y****o****u******

I felt a mixture of excitement and fear. Love is responsibility. He needed me. He needed me to respond; to say, "I love you too." I was aware that he could be tentatively waiting for my response. That this was not the time to play it cool.

And of course I wanted to reply. Of course I was eager to tell him how much I loved him too. Of course I wanted to cling on to this piece of happiness and never let go.

"I love you too ☺," I replied. And that was that. That's how quickly everything started.

Shortly afterwards I changed my Facebook status to "Hannah Wilson is in a relationship with Kyle Greer."

I got a zillion likes and comments for that status update. Friends, work colleagues, family; now everyone knew. We were official.

I wanted to shout it from the rooftops. I wanted to show off to everyone. I wanted to say, "See?! I am not a sad singleton! Someone does love me! I am not stuck on the shelf! I am wanted and loved and needed! So there!

Chapter Five

Kate

"Police are investigating the disappearance of local woman Hannah Greer from her home in Belfast. Mrs Greer, thirty-two, is five feet four inches in height, average build, with shoulder-length blonde hair. She was last seen on the morning of Monday 15 October by her husband, Kyle Greer."

"Mr Greer, interviewed by our reporters, has appealed to members of the public for any information possible."

"Oh my god! Did you hear that?" I say, setting down the kettle and looking over to Guy. He's sitting at the breakfast bar, piece of toast in one hand, holding onto the newspaper with the other.

"Hmm?"

"That news!" I say. "About the missing woman! Did you hear it?"

He looks up from the paper. "Sorry babe, I was miles away. What was it?"

I bring the now-boiled kettle to my cup and pour in the hot water. "There's a missing woman in Belfast. Hannah Somebody."

"Oh dear," he grimaces, but I can tell he's not really that interested.

I go to the fridge and take out the milk. All the while my mind is ticking over. I cock my head to one side.

"Hey, didn't you mention someone called Hannah in your work?" I muse.

He bites into his toast and murmurs. "Hmm, but I'm sure there's a million Hannahs in Belfast."

"True. Must check what her surname is again. I'll look it up online later."

Guy watches me as I clamber up onto the breakfast bar stool opposite him.

"So, any excitement planned for today?" he asks, a smile on his face.

He often asks me this in the morning. It's his way of checking in with me I guess, briefing my day.

"Got a business meeting this morning," I say, taking a piece of toast from the toast-tray and spreading it liberally with margarine. "Then a lunch meeting. Then back to the office for paperwork."

Guy grins at me. "You mean you'll have four large glasses of wine and roll home for a sleep."

I grin back. "I wish!" I pop my toast in my mouth and chew thoughtfully. My mind goes back to the missing woman. "I wonder what happened to her," I muse.

Guy looks at me quizzically, then cottons on to my line of thinking. "Oh, Hannah?" he replies. "Who knows!"

He seems uninterested in the story, but I can't let it go. I have visions of a creepy rapist doing the rounds in Belfast on the look-out for women in their thirties. And since I fall into that category, it freaks me out. I'll look it up online later and see if there's any way I can help. Maybe they'll organise a search walk for her.

"So what's your plans for the day?" I ask, anxious to change the subject as I'm aware I'm boring him.

His face crumples into a worried look. "Well, I'm battling on with another chapter today. Maybe even two if I can." He sighs and then adds, "Fingers crossed. This book will be the one."

I give Guy what I hope is a sympathetic smile. "Hey, I have every faith in you mister!"

"I know you do. You're my number one fan." Then he adds as an after-thought. "Probably my only fan, but hey-ho."

I give a little laugh. I know the whole writing thing really gets Guy down at times. His first book was successful enough – in as much as it got published. But it didn't earn

18

him the money he thought it would. Now he's trying to write a bestseller. One that a big publisher will take on board. He's still working part-time in an office doing accounts. But for the rest of the week, he's working from home on his book. I know that he feels guilty doing this. I know he hates that I'm the main breadwinner. But I joke with him and tell him not to be so sexist. I hope that my banter lightens the load for him.

Anyway we really don't need to worry financially. This house was left to me by my parents when they passed so it's not as if we have a crippling mortgage around our necks. As long as he contributes to the odd bill and buys the food shopping now and again, I'm happy. Besides, once he writes a bestseller and gets his foot on the literary ladder, we'll be rolling it in. And I'll be the proud partner of author Guy Jameson.

I catch my line of thinking. *Correction, I'm already the proud partner of author Guy Jameson.*

"Well babe, that's me. I better get a move on."

I stand up and give him a peck on the lips as I gather my bag and jacket together. I'm wearing a dark blue suit from Karen Millen and I just love the cut of it, it's so comfortable. And I have my new heels from Office. I adore them because they're comfy right from day one – no need to break them in. I spritz a bit of L'eau d'Issey, my favourite, and I'm off.

"Oh honey," I call, as I'm leaving. "If they do organise one of those search walks for Hannah, would you be up for joining me?"

Guy looks at me blankly. I can tell he hates the idea. Fresh air and walks are not his thing. He'd rather be stuck behind his computer, headphones on, listening to an audio book.

"Uh, sure," he replies, clearly saying yes for my benefit.

"Great! See you later! Happy writing!"

Chapter Six

Hannah

I wonder if I will end up like one of those Stockholm Syndrome cases where they're imprisoned and they actually start to enjoy being there.

As long as he doesn't come down and ask me questions or demand answers, I'm okay. As long as he brings me drugs and books, I'm okay. He's given me two books so far. One chick-lit and one psychological thriller. I'll get through these in no time.

He told me not to turn the page over at the top like a bookmark. I said 'as if!' I'd never do that to a book. He said that as long as the reading kept me quiet, that was okay by him. I think there used to be a TV in here once, but he took it out. He didn't want the sound of the TV travelling upstairs. I said I wouldn't have switched it on, but he said no. He said it would have been too tempting, during the long hours of boredom, to switch it on. There wasn't to be any sound.

Someone used to live in this basement. It has a sofa (which pulls out into a sofa-bed), a sink, running water, cupboards, and a toilet.

Maybe that's why I'm getting used to it; the home comforts. Or maybe it's the pills. Maybe the pills make me not care.

There's a part of me that really doesn't care. I'm okay with isolating. I had started to isolate, even before this. I had started to introvert all the time. Kyle said it was depression. I think he couldn't understand it; why I was depressed. I think he blamed himself.

It got to the stage where people would text me to arrange

meeting up and I'd groan. I couldn't be bothered to meet up. But how could I respond?

If I said, "Sure, that'd be lovely," out of politeness, they'd follow that up with another message arranging when we should meet. Then I'd have to go along and go through all the pleasantries when really I'd rather just be home in my own bed with a good book.

But I'd go along and smile and be nice and at the end of the get-together they'd say, "We must do this again sometime," and my heart would sink. But on the outside I'd smile and say, "Yeah, that'd be lovely." And the whole merry-go-round would continue.

The kind that got me was the people who chased after me. You see, the thing is, I think it should be give and take.

- Person #1 extends the invitation
- Person #2 accepts.

The next time it should be:

- Person #2 extends the invitation
- Person #1 accepts.

This shows an equal balance of both persons wanting to do the meeting up. But sometimes (especially with me), it was always Person #1 extending the invitation. And if I reluctantly accepted, inevitably they would go on to extend the invitation again without giving me the breathing space.

Kyle said that that was depression. But people don't *see* depression. People see you as being rude for not wanting to meet up.

So in some ways, it's like I'm trapped in this warm cocoon where I don't have to play at life. I don't have to meet people. I don't have to do anything. I can just lie here all day and take tablets and read books.

I wonder what's happening in the outside world. I wonder if the police are searching for me. I think back to Kyle's accusations. "You're depressed," he said. I think he saw it as a slight against him. As though it was his fault. As though how could our perfect relationship deteriorate so quickly?

I'm tired of thinking. Maybe I'll take some more tablets and read another chapter. Maybe by the time I'm halfway through the chapter, the tablets will put me to sleep.

Chapter Seven

Julia

I hug my scarf closer around my neck as I walk up the steep hill near Belfast Castle. I kick the autumnal leaves underfoot as I breathe in the fresh, crisp air. I love this time of year. The stuffy unbearableness of summer has passed. I hate all those people raving on about the great weather and all the wonderful things they can do with their kids – picnics in the park and days at the beach. The hot weather offends me. I'd much rather close the blinds and hide under a duvet on the sofa, reading a good book. But of course, if you do that in summer, you feel guilty. You feel like you should be out there, socialising, when it's the last thing you feel like doing.

At least I'm making an effort today, I think to myself, as I climb the hill towards the meeting point. My counsellor says that I should make an effort to help someone. She says that if I help someone, I'll feel better about myself. I doubt it. I mean, how can benefitting someone else make my situation better? But alas, I'll give it a go. I told her I was going to make an honest effort to follow her advice.

Today I'm helping a guy called Kyle. He's organised a search for his missing wife. It's pretty tragic really. The news about it has been everywhere – posts on Facebook, posters in pubs, posters in the shops, tweets, radio announcements. Everyone in Belfast knows about the #FindHannah campaign. I get the impression Kyle thinks the police aren't doing enough. Why else would he have put this appeal on Facebook for people to help find her?

We're doing a walk up Cave Hill. I guess the idea is that we're looking for any traces at all – her clothing, a scarf, a glove, and god forbid, her dead body.

That's not a status you want to put on Facebook – "Searching for a woman's dead body today." Doesn't really sound right. I did however post 'Joining in the #FindHannah campaign today', and then I checked myself in at Cave Hill, Belfast. I even posted a pretty autumnal picture of red and orange leaves which were scattered on the ground next to a tree.

I wonder if Tommy checks my Facebook anymore. I wonder if he stalks through the images to see if I've moved on; to see if there's a hunky man attached to my arm. Sadly, there isn't. I wonder if I could sidle up to some bloke in the walk today and take a sneaky selfie. I don't have to say anything. It could be a cryptic clue that I might have moved on to fresh pastures. That always makes men come running back, doesn't it? When they spot on the radar that you're no longer pining after them they rush back for a second chance.

I breathe in the fresh autumnal air and try to breathe out any thoughts of Tommy. The counsellor was right. This fresh air is wonderful. I see a small crowd gathering up ahead and realise this must be the #FindHannah crew. As I get closer again, I can spot Kyle. I've never met him before but I recognise him from his Facebook photos. He's 'Facebook Famous' as my brother would say.

"Hi," I smile shyly as I approach him. "You're Kyle?" I ask, an unnecessary question. "I'm Julia. I'm here to help."

I'm here to help. I cringe. It's nearly as bad as 'I carried a watermelon.' I sound like either Baby from Dirty Dancing or like a corny sales assistant in an American retail shop.

But Kyle seems unperturbed by my corniness. Instead he flashes a grateful smile. "Julia!" he says triumphantly, as though I'm a long-lost friend. "Thank you so much for coming!"

I smile back, touched by his gratitude. My tone then changes into what I hope is a respectful sympathy. "I'm so sorry for what you're going through. You must be a nervous wreck."

I nearly said, 'I'm so sorry for your loss.' I'm so glad I

24

didn't. It was on the tip of my tongue. It's that cliché phrase that everyone says. But 'loss' would've assumed she's dead. How disrespectful would it have been to say that?

Already I'm wishing I could crawl back to the comfy confines of my sofa. All this awkwardness isn't worth it.

But Kyle puts me at ease. "Thank you," he says. His eyes genuinely look grateful. "I haven't had much sleep, I'll be honest. But I'm so grateful for all the support I've been getting. People are coming out of the woodwork to help, it's lovely."

He gives me that warm smile again. I know it's really inappropriate, but I can't help but notice how good-looking he is. I did notice it on his photos of course but in person – I dunno – he's just so warm and charismatic. I know it's the biggest cliché in the book, but he really is looking at me as though I'm the only girl in the room (or should I say, the only girl on this hilltop).

I expect that when everyone sets off walking, I'll lose him in the crowd and I'll just become one of the numbers. But that doesn't happen. He walks beside me all along the way. I don't know if I'm imagining it but there does seem to be an invisible bond between us – a magnetic pull. People have told me in the past that I'm a good listener and I wonder if it's that. I wonder if he's enjoying having a shoulder to cry on, someone who'll actually listen and not butt in and steer the conversation back to them. He's telling me about the day she went missing, how that he sensed it straight away. How that she's always home at the same time every day and if she'll be late, she'll always text. He said about the police, how they questioned him for ages but still haven't come up with anything. And how he decided to take matters into his own hands and organise a search himself.

Someone calls over at him at that point. "Kyle! Could this be anything?"

He spins around quickly to see one of the volunteers holding up a hat. Rushing over, he assesses the hat. It's a woman's flat cap in a pale grey colour. But I can see his immediate hope turning into quick resignation.

"No," he says. "I've never seen her wearing a hat like this. She wears woolly hats the odd time but never these."

"Sorry mate," the volunteer says.

Kyle pats him on the arm gratefully. "Thanks though," he smiles warmly.

The search continues for several hours. To be honest, I think most of us are enjoying the walk. We're lucky to get a nice day and although the air is nippy, we're wrapped up well. Plus the hours of walking brings the body temperature up. People are chatting amongst themselves and new friendships are being formed.

We've had several sightings – a hat here, a glove there, but nothing that resembles any of Hannah's clothes according to Kyle. And the unspoken word of course is that no dead bodies have been found. This is both a good thing and a bad thing. The point of the search was to find something – something that would bring some resolution to this case. Something that would ease Kyle's mind. But surely not finding anything is a better sign. Surely that means she's still out there – hopefully alive.

When darkness begins to fall, Kyle decides to call off the search. Although a few people have left already, making their apologies, some persistent stragglers have remained. Kyle thanks everyone profusely for their help and for staying on so long. He asks everyone if they'll keep in touch.

As the crowd disperses, Kyle watches them go, a look across his face that I can't put my finger on – gratitude? Guilt?

I place a reassuring hand on his arm. "We'll find her," I say. "We will. She has to be out there somewhere."

He smiles gratefully. "I just wish there was some way I could repay you all. I feel so guilty taking up everyone's time."

"Don't be silly!" I scoff, in what I hope is a playful light tone. "People are happy to help."

He thrusts his hands into his pockets and moves his body on the balls of his feet. "I guess so," he says. Then he adds, "It's getting kinda chilly now. Do you fancy a cuppa to warm up? There's a café just there." He points to the grand Belfast castle at the foot of Cave Hill.

I'm surprised by his offer, but I immediately reply, "Sure! That'd be lovely! As we walk together towards the café, I'm dying to take a selfie of us, but of course I refrain. I need to play it cool. How much would it piss Tommy off though if he saw this? It'd be like putting the middle finger up to him and saying, "So there!"

The warmth of the café hits me the moment I enter. A fire crackles in an open grate. There's a low murmur of other patrons quietly drinking their tea. The décor is oldie-worldly – antique furniture and low beams and candles flickering in used wine bottles.

"Oh, it's lovely in here," I say aloud, rubbing my gloved hands together and appreciating the warmth.

Kyle nods in agreement and peruses their display case. "Fancy a scone as well?" he asks.

"Hmm, good idea," I agree, feeling like we're on a first date rather than an impromptu coffee.

"You take a seat," Kyle says authoritatively. "I'll order and bring it down."

"Oh… okay," I say, caught on the hoof. "Here, let me give you some money for mine…" I begin, reaching into my bag for my purse. But before I'm even finishing my sentence, he's waving that notion away like a fly.

"Please," he says. "It's the least I can do after you've trekked all these hours for me."

Slowly I oblige and trot off to find us a spot. I locate a table near to the fire and settle myself down. I look around, feeling somewhat smug with myself. *Get me. I'm out and about. I'm not on my sofa. How proud will my counsellor be?*

I take a sneaky picture of the open fire and upload it onto Instagram. I add #cosyfire #autumnaldays #coffee #scones.

Maybe later, if Kyle nips to the loo, I'll get a photo of the two empty cups and empty plates. I can already picture the heading I'll use. #enjoyedthat #allgone

"Now," Kyle says, as he returns with a tray. "Scones it is." He sets a plate with a huge scone in front of me along with

27

the cutest little jar of jam and a pot of fresh cream.

#DayMade.

Tucking into the jam and cream, we both spread the scones liberally and make small talk about how nice it is to get into the warmth.

Then Kyle begins to open up in a more deep and meaningful way. He tells me about how guilty he feels – that all these people have taken hours out of their precious time off to join in a search party. I reassure him that they'd be happy to help.

"I suppose that's the one good thing about social media," I comment. "You get to reach out to those kind souls that are happy to help."

Kyle nods. Then he flashes me a warm smile which I can't help but read as flirtatious.

"So is that what you are?" he asks, the hint of a devilish smile crossing his lips. "A kind soul happy to help?"

I feel my cheeks flush with embarrassment. "Oh no, that's not what I was saying…" I begin my earnest protest.

But he playfully interrupts me. "Aw, I'm only kiddin' ya, I knew what you meant."

It's at that moment that a little alarm bell rings in the back of my mind. A little tinkle of an alarm bell that says, *'Is this normal? For a devastated husband of a missing wife to be making jokes?'* But I brush that thought away. And just then a waitress passes with a kind smile and a coffee pot, asking if we want a top-up.

I remind myself how lucky I am, to be out and about, sitting next to an open fire and a handsome man, doing my good deed for the day and being part of life.

"Oh, yes please," Kyle coos at the waitress. And then I realise, it's just the way he is; charming, charismatic, jovial. He's hardly going to be miserable to everyone and take his worry out on them.

We chat further. Kyle asks about me, my job, where I live and if I'm single.

I almost choke at the last question. It seems so forward but he asks it with such an air of normality, as though he's asking my shoe size.

"Yeah, I am actually," I reply. I wait for the pitying look, for the patronising comments such as; *'aw, such a shame, nice girl like you?'* etc, but they don't come.

Instead he nods his head as though this is perfectly normal and says, "You've more sense then?" He gives me a little wink.

"Yup!" I agree, with rather more forced joviality than intended. "It's great to have the place to myself!"

He nods and smiles. "No bloke leaving a messy bathroom."

"Or laundry basket," I agree, smiling.

"Where do you live?" he asks. "I mean, I'm not asking for your actual address or anything, just the general area."

I laugh. "East Belfast."

"Near me then."

I smile awkwardly, not sure what to say to that. Is he implying we'll be seeing each other again?

And then the awkward silence is broken when he looks at his watch and says, "Shit! Is that the time? I need to head on."

"Oh, sure!" The sudden change in atmosphere has puzzled me but I tell myself not to be so uptight. He probably has loads of calls to make to keep people informed on how the walk went.

"I'll just dash to the loo first," he says.

And when he's gone, I take a photo of our empty cups, plates and jam jars. I make sure the open fire is in the background of the shot, upload it to Instagram, add a filter and write the comment "#daysout #BelfastCastle #autumn #cosy."

Chapter Eight

Kerry

"So, what's our motives?" Simon asks as he stands at the whiteboard and faces us.

A group of us are gathered in the meeting room; me, Barry, Peter and of course, Simon. We've all been assigned to the case of the missing Hannah Greer, along with a pile of other cases.

"Money?" I ask. "They seem pretty wealthy. Lovely big house and rich interior. Maybe she's being held somewhere in return for a ransom?"

"Very good, Kerry. Yes, money," he says, scrawling the word at the top of the board.

"Sex?" I say. This seems weird, as though I'm asking Simon for sex, so I quickly follow this up with; "Perhaps a rapist or sex offender, holding her for his personal gain?"

"You're on the ball today Kerry. Yep, sex," he says loudly, scrawling it across the board.

"Jealousy?" Barry pipes up. "Maybe she's got an enemy somewhere that we don't know about?"

"Need to speak to the husband about that one. See if he knows anything," Simon agrees.

"Or speak to her work colleagues?" I suggest. "Maybe there's someone in work that the husband doesn't know about?"

"True," Simon acknowledges. Then Simon turns to the board and scrawls 'Love.' "There's always this of course. The husband may well be our suspect. Just because he made the call, doesn't mean he's innocent. In fact..." Simon continues, twirling his pen in his hand as he faces us, "... as you well know, often it's the person closest to the victim that's to blame. Let's just say he's our suspect. What if he's harmed her, then hidden her. He could have phoned in and pronounced her as a missing person just to throw us off the scent."

As I'm watching Simon, I can't help but be distracted by his pen twirling, by the curve of his biceps under his shirt. I immediately reprimand myself for being so girlish. I'm here on a potential murder case for god's sake, not to admire a bloke like some sort of teenage crush.

"We're gonna have to search the house," Simon says. "I've arranged a search warrant, but we need to handle this carefully. It's going to get his back up if he knows we suspect him." He suddenly calls my name. "Kerry. I want you to come out with me today. You're familiar with the case and you know how to handle him."

I feel my cheeks redden slightly as I'm aware of the other officers looking at me. I'm sure they're green with envy that I'm being picked as if I'm the golden child. I'm brimming with pride but trying not to show it. All I can do is think of how I'm going to tell my mum about this. How proud she'll be.

"Plan of action is," Simon continues, obviously unaware of the rollercoaster of thoughts whirring around in my head. "We'll go round to talk to him but we need to keep him on our side initially. We need to ask him about the money thing – any known enemies, any jealous friends. Find out if he's had any threats for money – although I'm sure he would have told us that by now if that was the case. Then we need to tread carefully with the search warrant. He's not gonna like it so Kerry, you need to try to work some magic on him. Keep him calm. Just tell him that this is a routine procedure. We have to search all areas that Hannah would've circulated in before we move on to a greater area. So obviously home and work are our first port of calls."

I give a small smile.

"Peter, Barry," he motions to two other officers. "I need you both on standby in the car and we'll beckon you in when we need help with the search."

They nod.

"Okay! Let's go!" Simon instructs, obviously fired up with adrenalin. "Bet that bugger has her locked in the basement or something."

Chapter Nine

<u>Hannah</u>

The chinks in the armour started to show as early at the honeymoon. Imagine that. The ring was only on my finger one day.

I should have known that something suspicious was in the air when his mother made that comment to me on our wedding day.

"I don't know what you're smiling about," she grimaced, when I was standing there in my beautiful white dress waiting to greet people before dinner. "All he's done is taken you off the shelf and put you in front of the kitchen sink."

A small gasp escaped from my throat. I couldn't believe she had the nerve to be so bitchy, so vindictive. But she said it with a hint of a smirk on her face, as though she thought she was being funny.

I wanted to say, "Err, bit of an inappropriate joke?" But of course I said nothing. I was playing the blushing bride; virginal and pure; polite and elegant.

I seethed inside though, knocking back that first glass of Prosecco with gusto, cursing the fact that this witch was now going to be my mother-in-law for the rest of my life.

The rest of my life. Funny how I thought that.

The next day we were being led to our hotel room by the bell-boy. He was friendly and pleasant, chatting amiably. I chatted back, jovial and happy, delighted to be in a hot country on our honeymoon; our idyllic blissful honeymoon.

After the bellboy had gone and the door slammed of its own accord behind him, Kyle hissed at me, "Could you be any more flirty?" His face was thunderous.

I gulped in surprise. I'd never seen this anger in him before.

"What…?" I stammered, unsure of what he meant. I was friendly to the guy yes, but flirtatious?

"How do you think it makes me feel when my own wife is flirting with the staff?" His frown deepened, his shoulders hunched.

"Oh Kyle, I wasn't flirting!" I reached out to place a comforting hand on his arm, but he shrugged me away.

"I'm taking a shower," he said sternly, indicating the conversation was over.

I sat on the hotel chair, listening to the water pelting the shower-tray and my thoughts whirred.

Had that really happened? Had he really taken such offence? I blinked back tears. Could this really be happening on our honeymoon?

When he emerged from the bathroom, his mood was quiet. He reclined on the bed and switched on the TV. The sound of a football match grated on my nerves, so I went into the bathroom and ran a bath.

Lying in the deep tub, the bubbles caressing me gently, the shrill noise from the football match ruined any pampering feeling. Day one of our honeymoon and we had seemed to reach a silent impasse.

***

It's funny how the abnormal slowly turns into the normal. Well, funny isn't really the appropriate word. Funny, peculiar. Funny, strange.

After the bell-boy incident, I learned never to be overly friendly to other men. Never to be friendly at all actually. I was all one-word answers and frosty responses to men, when Kyle was around.

I made up excuses for him. I told myself that it wasn't his fault that he was jealous and insecure. I reminded myself that he'd had a difficult upbringing. That his father had been a violent alcoholic. That he had to endure many beatings at the hand of an alcohol-fuelled father. I told myself that it was no wonder he was insecure. I also reasoned with myself that I had no interest in flirting with other men, that Kyle was the only man I wanted, so what harm was it to act distant with other men.

We had gone down to dinner that evening – day one of our honeymoon.

After the football, he'd turned off the TV and fallen asleep. A nap seemed to help perk him up because during dinner, he was in better form. We ate delicious food and drank exquisite wine. He chatted as though nothing had happened earlier that day – as though no cross words had ever been spoken. I did, however, remember not to be over-friendly to our waiter. In fact, I don't even think I made eye-contact with him. I simply stated what food I wanted and that was that. No other chit-chat.

Kyle clinked glasses with me. "To us," he crooned.

"To us," I repeated, desperate to erase our earlier tension and start afresh.

"Aww, I feel so much better after that nap," he stated. "I think the hot weather really tired me out."

I smiled. Surely this was his way of apologising. Of blaming his crotchety bad mood on the stuffy climate.

But that was the problem, I started to realise. Every time there was one incident, I'd tell myself that that would be the last. His mood would lift, everything would seem okay again, and I'd convince myself that that was just a blip, that it would never happen again.

The real problem would occur when I let my guard down. When I'd forget to be mindful. Sometimes I'd just react or say something mean, or be argumentative, and I'd forget, like the time I whined about wanting children.

We had only been married a few months, so I guess I was being really impatient. With each month, my hopes were dashed when the red streak appeared on my knickers.

"I wonder if we should get tested," I said aloud. I really didn't mean anything bad about it. I was just wondering. Wondering if we were both fertile. He didn't take it well though. He seemed to see it as some sort of slight against his manliness or something.

His chair scraped back, and he stood up abruptly. It was so fast that his chair crashed back and hit the tiled floor. He stormed out of the kitchen and stomped up the stairs.

I sat there in shock, my heart hammering. What? What did I say? My mind whirled.

I wondered if I should follow him upstairs and talk to him about it. But I was too scared. His mood was thick; black. I thought it best to let him stew for a while, let him cool down.

But I couldn't relax. It was as if I was creeping around the house on eggshells.

Should I adopt a pose of relaxed reading in the conservatory? Or would that look like I didn't care?

Should I don washing up gloves and clean the house manically?

Or should I just disappear – leave the house and grab a friend and hit a wine bar?

Oh, how I wanted to do the latter. But I felt that wouldn't be appropriate either. In the end, I opted for the manic cleaning. It seemed more fitting somehow, as though I was punishing myself for being so thoughtless.

There was something therapeutic about the cleaning actually. It calmed my mind. The way that the cloth rubbed along the windows. The way that the streaks became smaller and smaller until the glass gleamed spotless. It helped me to switch off. I knew that if he did come into the room and saw me cleaning, he would give me an approving nod and leave the room. Whereas if I was sprawled along the sofa, watching a daytime T.V. talk-show, cuppa in one hand, chocolate bar in the other, he would look at me with disdain, as though I was a waste of space.

No, I knew that cleaning was the safer option. Cleaning didn't elicit a rolled eye or bad atmosphere.

But even that wasn't a safe option after a while. Even after all my cleaning, it seemed that I still missed spots. One day, when he was in a particularly bad mood, he called me to the bathroom.

"Look at this!" he said, pointing to a spot behind the door.

I felt my heart beating wondering what on earth had gotten him so angry. Had a phantom dog crept in through the window, taken a shit, and then left?

I looked but could see nothing.

"What is it?" I asked.

He sighed as though pointing out an easy maths equation to a child.

"Look further," he demanded, his voice like thunder. His hand was on the small of my back, pushing me further.

I leaned further, my insides crawling with humiliation. And then I spotted it, a small clump of dust, gathered in the corner, like a sleeping spider.

"Oh," I responded.

"Yes, oh," he repeated, his tone sarcastic and mimicking me. "Clearly you're not doing the cleaning properly if you're missing bits."

I should have shrugged and said, "And what? Pay a cleaner then if you want the place to be perfect! What did your last skivvy die of?"

But that's not what happens unfortunately. What happens is that you go into a state of shock. You can hardly believe that this man is talking to you like this. This man, who claims to love you and cherish you, who at one stage worshipped the ground you walked on, now seems to despise you.

But also you know that it's temporary, that one minute he'll be letting off steam about a bit of dust, and then the next, he'll be acting like nothing happened. He'll be eating the dinner you cooked him and commenting on how delicious it tastes. He'll be snuggling up to you on the sofa and acting like no harsh words were ever said. It's as if he is struck down with temporary amnesia.

You become the Queen of Excuses. You excuse him relentlessly. You tell yourself that he's tired or stressed. That he's had a bad day at the office and he's not aware of his bad mood.

You tell yourself that if you don't react, this situation will quietly pass.

You certainly don't react or retaliate. If you were to retaliate, that would only make him angrier and blow the whole situation out of proportion.

So you go into switch-off mode. You turn your emotions off. It's as if you're outside of yourself watching the situation. You watch as you go to the kitchen and get the dustbin and brush. You watch as you get on your knees and scoop the godforsaken piece of dust off the silly floor. You watch him as he's watching you. He's standing there, with that smug look of being in control. The power going straight to his tiny balls.

And then it's over. For now. And even though it's over, your soul has quietly retreated a little more inside of you. The spark has gotten that little bit smaller. And the love has shrunken just that fraction more.

***

In some ways I was dying to talk to someone about it. To tell them about my new husband. To confide that perhaps this was a huge mistake. How had I judged him so incorrectly? How had I thought he was the love of my life when actually now I wasn't so sure of who he even was anymore?

But who could I tell? Who could I confide in?

I didn't want to tell my mum or sisters. They would only worry sick about me. They might even turn up at the door and demand to chop his balls off.

And I didn't want to tell my friends. Many of them were newly married themselves. Loved up. Expecting babies.

Okay, I'll be honest. The reason I didn't want to tell anyone was pride. What would they think of me?

They'd think I was a pathetic walk over, someone who couldn't stand up for herself.

They'd encourage me to leave him. I might even have to end up living back in my parent's house again. I could NOT live in my parent's house again. I could not be that sad singleton at the age of thirty who lives with their parents.

I could not be the poor lonely girl who couldn't even survive a year of marriage.

So yeah, I'll be honest, my pride was a problem. What's that saying, about pride before a fall? That's me.

Pride and excuses. Maybe it'll be different next time. Maybe this is a one-off. Maybe if this situation passes quietly, we'll just get back to normal. Maybe he's just stressed. Maybe it's just a bad day.

But there was one person I could talk to, I suppose. My friend at work, Guy. He had a way of sussing out my moods. He could tell when I was anxious, when I was stressed, or when I had something on my mind.

I suppose that's what happens when you spend so much time in someone's company, when they're looking across at you from the next desk. When they share the same coffee-dock, the same canteen.

"Hannah?" he'd said one day, when we were the only two in the coffee dock.

I looked over at him, those kind enquiring brown eyes, the sympathetic look on his face.

"Is everything okay?" he'd enquired.

I wondered if he heard my heart thumping. I wondered if he spotted how wide my pupils were dilating. I wondered if he'd noticed that I felt like he was looking inside my soul.

"Yeah, why…?" I trailed off, sounding as unconvincing as I felt.

He looked a tad uncomfortable then, as though he knew he was crossing the line. "I dunno…It's just that, you seem a lot quieter today, I just wondered if everything was okay…." He trailed off. "Sorry, you don't have to say if…"

"No, it's fine," I interrupted softly. "Thank you for asking, but I'm fine, honestly." My heart warmed to him like marshmallows melting next to an open fire.

He looked at me, relief on his face evident. "I didn't mean to pry. I just…"

"Honestly," I affirmed sweetly. "I'd tell you if there was anything wrong."

I could tell he didn't believe me. "Okay."

And I would tell him. Maybe. One day. Just not today. Not yet.

Chapter Ten

Julia

"Thanks again," Kyle says as we walk out of the coffee shop and out into the cool air.

I pull my scarf closer around my neck, hugging it to me. "Thank *you* for the coffee," I say. "That was lovely."

"It was." He agrees. I can't place the look on his face. Amusement? Gratitude? Or dare I suggest it, attraction?

I smile, awkwardly, not sure where to look.

As though picking up on my shyness, he compliments me. "You're very easy to talk to. You're a good listener."

Actually, I'm not going to argue with him there. People have often said that I'm a good listener. I used to think that was such a boring compliment. As though it meant that I had nothing much to say for myself. That I'd just be happy to sit there and let the other person do the talking. But now I'm not so sure. I've chatted to people who won't let you get a word in edgeways and actually it's quite annoying. And anyway, my counsellor says I'm to take a compliment graciously and accept that I do have good points.

"Maybe you're easy to listen to," I find myself saying. Goodness me! I even have a flirtatious tone in my voice.

Kyle smiles, a twinkle in his eye. "I must get your number," he says casually, as though an afterthought. Pulling his phone out of his pocket, he unlocks the screen and fiddles about with the keypad whilst casually continuing his pick-up line. "We could get another coffee sometime or…"

"Sure!" I say, realising I've responded too quickly. Why can't I ever play it cool? I mentally kick myself.

He hands over his phone, silently ushering for me to type

my number into his phone. I pray my hands don't shake, which sometimes happens when I'm nervous. But thankfully, my blessed hands stay still and I return the phone to him, job done.

He nods his head in the direction of his car. "D'you need a lift home?"

I shake my head and swivel my body in the direction of my own little beat-up. "Ah no. It's cool. I'm driving."

He gives me that intimate smile again. "Well thanks again Julia. I hope to see you soon."

"Yeah, me too."

And then I'm off, heading towards my car, hoping that I don't suddenly trip over a broken branch in my departure.

Of course, the minute I get in the car and begin my drive home, my head starts with the anxious thoughts.

What are you thinking, Julia? The thoughts say.

Do you honestly believe he would be interested in you?

May I remind you that he's looking for his dead wife?

I switch on my window wipers as a light splattering of rain begins to hit the windscreen. If only the gentle 'swish, swish' of the wipers could wipe my paranoid thoughts away. Arriving home, I head to the kitchen and open the fridge. I know what will wipe the anxiety away. Taking a bottle of wine that I had mercifully left in the fridge door for chilling, I take the corkscrew and hear the welcome 'pop' followed by the 'glug, glug, glug' as it hits the side of the glass.

I take a sweep of my apartment, turning on the lamps and closing the blinds. Peeling off my daytime clothes and unhooking my bra, I pull on my comfy pyjamas and hit the sofa. I reach over and take the single duvet that's folded up on the armchair. Stretching it over me, I take the remote control and switch on the TV. I need to switch on some reality TV and switch off my head.

Glass of wine in one hand, remote in the other, I start to feel myself relaxing. As the wine begins to trickle down to my toes, enveloping me in a soft, warm, fuzziness, I instantly begin to feel better. Several glasses of wine later, any earlier anxiety has dissipated and in its place is a glow of contentment. I notice that my thoughts move from anxiety to quiet self-congratulation.

Didn't I do well to get out and about today?

Get me ending up on an impromptu coffee date!

And he even took my number and wants to meet up again!

As if reading my thoughts, I hear the 'bleep, bleep' of my phone. Looking down, I see that it's a text from Kyle.

Hey. Thanks again for all your help today. And for the listening ear ☺ Coffee soon? xx

I gulp. Jeepers, I wasn't expecting a text from him so quickly. I know I should be playing it cool, but I reply straight away. I can't help it. I'm blaming the wine for my laissez-faire attitude.

Absolutely. Or even a bite to eat. I'm a mean cook if I say so myself ;) xx

The 'bleep, bleep' reply bounces back immediately.

I'm gonna take you up on that! ☺ Tomorrow night? ;) xx

I gulp and sit upright, suddenly slightly sobered up by the implications of his text.

He wants to come around for dinner tomorrow night?!

That means a herculean planning operation which needs to be implemented immediately:

a.Plan what I will cook.

b.Go to the supermarket tomorrow morning to buy the ingredients.

c.Go to the hairdressers to get a wash and blow-dry (it's essential – my hair won't sit right otherwise).

d.Have a shower and Veet and shave (Yes, I know – that sounds presumptuous but really it's just a cautionary step).

e.Put on a nice outfit and do my make-up.

f.COOK THE DAMN THING!

I can feel myself hyperventilating at the very thought of it. Why did I have to act like the big girl? Why couldn't I just have agreed to a quick coffee and leave it at that?

I take another huge sip of my wine. Gawd, I could drink the rest of the bottle at this rate!

This is what happens when you venture out of your comfort blanket! I think. *You end up agreeing to cook for a complete stranger twenty-four hours later!*

As though reading my thoughts, I hear the 'bleep, bleep' of my phone again.

It'd be really lovely to chat to you again. It's lovely to meet someone with such a listening ear. Especially at this difficult time xx

Gawd, now I have to agree. He's given me the potentially dead wife card.

Taking a deep breath, I tap out my response

No problem, it'd be great to see you too xx

Then I type out my address details, give a time, and hit send.

***

I decide on a lamb moussaka with chips. It's easy. I've made it a million times and I can't go wrong. Now is not the time to experiment with a new dish. I've been to the supermarket. I've bought the ingredients. And I buy a simple shop-made dessert. If he thinks I'm spending time baking a dessert, he'll have another think coming. I need to try to make this day as simple as I can. So I've shopping bought, hair done and showered. I cook the moussaka and I'm grateful to have something to do with my hands. The repetitive chopping, whipping and stirring is helping to calm my nerves. I also pop a little beta-blocker to slow my heart rate down a little. Needs must.

It's way too early but I decide to get dressed and do my make-up anyway. Once I know that absolutely everything is ready, then I can sit and relax. All I'll have to do is warm the moussaka up just before he arrives.

I opt for a smart casual outfit. I'm wearing a short skirt, black tights and a knitted top. I wear my snug slippers and hope that the final look is cutesy and autumnal. I keep my make-up light and natural. I don't want to seem like I'm trying too hard.

He's married Julia, remember?

He has a wife who is missing, possibly dead, remember?

I pop another little pill for good measure and then sit and watch TV for a while, trying not to overthink the evening ahead.

When I hear the knock of the door later, I jump. It is loud and forceful, manly even. It's been a long time since a man has come knocking to my door, I realise.

I open the door and see him standing there, a bottle of wine in one hand, a bunch of flowers in the other.

"Hello!" I say warmly. "Come in, come in!" I stand back to let him pass me in the hallway, immediately struck by the scent of his manly aftershave. Is that Calvin Klein? I'm not sure.

"It smells nice," he says, obviously referring to my cooking.

"Oh," I give a light chuckle. "I hope it tastes as good as it smells!"

He gives me a warm smile. "I'm sure it will."

It feels like time pauses for a brief moment as we're stood there, looking at each other. He's wearing a dark brown jumper and dark jeans. Towering over me, he looks handsome and smells so nice. I have to remind myself that this is not a date. That I am simply a sympathetic friend who is a shoulder to cry on.

"Oh!" he says, "these are for you." He holds the flowers and wine towards me.

"Oh! Thank you, they're lovely." I can't remember the last time a man bought flowers for me. Well I can, it was Tommy. But that was ages ago, and why the hell am I even thinking about Tommy right now? He's the last person I want in my head.

There's the initial settling period where I offer him to sit down. I pour a glass of wine for him and fiddle about with putting the flowers in a vase whilst he sits on the sofa chatting with me.

He tells me he's had a hellish day. That's there's still no news on Hannah, that the police are being pretty useless and that he feels it must be low on their list of priorities.

"They keep telling me that they're doing everything in their power to find her, but I don't believe that for one minute," he says.

I give him a sympathetic look. "Did they say what exactly they are doing?"

"No, I think they interviewed a few people – went to her workplace, tried to get some leads, but that's about the height of it."

"Well fair play to you," I say. "You've obviously got the press involved in it because there's news about her everywhere."

"Hmm, thank god for social media I suppose."

I set the vase of flowers on the table. "They're so lovely," I say, admiring them. I'm not sure if I'm subconsciously trying to move the subject away from Hannah.

"Food coming up." I smile brightly, as I disappear back into the kitchen.

"You have a lovely home."

"Oh thanks!" I call back, bustling about the kitchen with my oven gloves and serving spoon. "It's pretty modest but it does me. And I've made it as cosy as I can."

"It's cute," he agrees, obviously taking in the pink fairy lights, the canvas pictures displaying pink hearts and cute kittens.

I bring the steaming plates of food to the dining table and usher for him to join me. "Please, eat."

"This looks delicious!" he says, appreciatively, sitting down at the table and picking up his cutlery. "It seems like ages since I've had a decent meal!"

"Has it been cuppa soups and carry-outs?" I tease gently.

He grins. "Yeah, something like that, I'll admit."

He tucks in and genuinely seems to enjoy it. We chat amiably and discuss the normal topics – work and what it is we both do. It seems Kyle is the owner of some sort of printing business. They make signs or something. I think he is downplaying his role, but it sounds like he's the manager of about thirty employees. I feel somewhat embarrassed to tell him about my meagre secretarial job, but he encourages me.

"Hey, if you enjoy it and it pays the bills, then it's all good!"

"Hmm," I don't exactly enjoy my job, but I don't really want to go into that now. "Do you enjoy yours?" I ask, as usual wanting to deflect the conversation on to the other person.

"Enjoy? Hmm, I wouldn't go that far, but it's good money and I'm my own boss, so yeah, it works." He gives me that lovely smile again and I can feel my insides melt.

I thought I was going to be a nervous wreck tonight but now that he's here, I've no time to be nervous. I'm in the moment, listening to his stories, busying myself with the food and then clearing the dishes into the kitchen, that I've no time to feel nerves. Added to that, the wine that he brought with him is absolutely superb. I've no idea where he bought it or how much it cost but it's bloody delicious!

"Do you smoke?" he asks, a cheeky grin on his face.

"Smoke? I …"

He produces a small tin from his pocket and opens it. I'm suddenly aware then that he's not discussing cigarettes. He has brought some dope with him.

"Oh, I…" I'm lost for words for some reason. I'm no prude but it's been a long time since I've been offered a spliff. I don't normally allow smoking in my home, but it seems a bit prudish to say no. "Oh, okay…"

I have a momentarily panicky thought. What if the police suddenly called at my door? What if they receive news about Hannah and need to get in touch with Kyle? What if by some miracle they found out that he was at mine? What would they say about dope?

I swipe that thought away in my head, telling myself not to be so ridiculous. As if they would turn up at my house. I'm just being paranoid.

Kyle effortlessly rolls the joint. I can tell this is a regular thing for him. I have to admit, it smells nice. Soothing. And it feels great. After only a few tokes, I can feel myself relaxing like butter melting on a stove.

Before I know it, I'm curled along my sofa like a contented cat. Kyle is curled along the other end. Our legs are touching. He's looking at me with that soft, easy stare. Holding my gaze, smiling at me.

"It's so funny how we met," he says. "How you just popped into my life at the right time."

"Yeah, it is."

"You're like an angel who came along to help me at the right time."

I playfully hit his leg with the tip of my toe. "You're full of shit," I tease.

He laughs in agreement. But he holds his stare and then his face becomes serious. "I mean it though."

I gulp, feeling the intensity of the moment.

Somehow he's sitting upright, and somehow his face is close to mine. And somehow I'm wanting him to kiss me. I'm not thinking about anything else. I'm just thinking about how close his face is to mine, about how intense his gaze is, about how the air is thick with tension.

And then he's kissing me. Soft, light kisses where his tongue is lightly playing with mine. And then later, more intense, as his tongue plunges further into my mouth, as though drinking me in, as though wanting to eat me.

"Julia," he groans, between kisses.

And I'm lost.

Chapter Eleven

Kate

"I can't believe I managed to get you out of the house today," I joke with Guy. I know full-well that he'd rather be tucked up in his little office, camped behind his computer. I don't know how he does it. Hours and hours of being in the same little space. When there's a great big world out there, waiting to be explored.

We're walking up Cave Hill to help with the #FindHannah campaign. And thankfully it's a gorgeous day. Even though summer has passed and we're edging towards the winter and the dark nights, we've been lucky enough to catch a clear and crisp autumn day. I breathe in the fresh air, letting it fill my lungs. How lovely it is to get out of the office! I adore the sound of the leaves crisping underfoot.

Guy jokes back. "I'm not that bad, am I? You make it out like I'm some night-time vampire."

"Well, aren't you?" I jest.

"Yes," he says, placing his hands around my waist and, in a mock-cartoon voice, says, "And I will come and bite you in zee middle of zee night."

I giggle and then quickly stop myself.

"Shush," I whisper realising that this is inappropriate. We're on a walk to help find a missing person, not to have flirty banter.

"Sorry," he whispers.

I look ahead and spot Kyle a few yards up. So far we have found nothing but I'm still glad I'm helping. I can't imagine what that poor man is going through.

"He must be at his wit's end," I say. "I mean, one day

she's there, and everything's fine, and then the next, disappeared. I mean, how can that happen?"

Guy runs his hand through his hair. "Well, it can easily happen, that's the point. It happens all the time, doesn't it?"

"Yeah, I guess. It's just you know... it just seems so shocking... when it's practically on your doorstep."

"Well...," says Guy. "I did tell you, didn't I, that it is the same Hannah I worked with?"

I look over at him. "No, you didn't mention that! Oh my god! How awful!"

Guy purses his lips. "I know. It's horrible."

"Did the police contact your work? Have there been any enquiries?"

Guy shrugs his shoulders. "I dunno. I suppose cos I'm only there part-time. I won't find out until I'm next in. But I imagine they will come in and talk to us all yeah."

We continue walking, and there is a moment of comfortable silence. I'm thinking about the kind of things the police will ask them. I'm looking at the beautiful view – the clear blue sky, the green fields, the orange and red leaves. I'm thinking about Hannah, wondering where she is. Probably cooped up in some rapist's den somewhere. I pull my coat tighter around me, hugging myself in comfort.

"They'll probably ask about the people at work. If she has any enemies or anything. Anyone who's jealous of her." I realise that in my thinking aloud, I'm actually asking Guy these questions. Does he know of anyone at their work? Any creepy men who had an obsession with her? Any jealous females who had it in for Hannah?

Guy seems to be musing over my question, as though shining a metaphorical spotlight on his colleagues. "Hmm, I really don't think so," he says. "I mean, everyone liked Hannah. You couldn't not really."

I raise an eyebrow. "Why's that?"

I can't help but feel a twinge of jealousy. Did Guy find her attractive? Then I immediately scold myself for being so ridiculous. Imagine being jealous of a missing woman who's probably locked in some rapist's den!

"Well she was just one of those placid people, you know? The type who just put the head down, got on with her work. Pleasant enough if you chatted to her, but she kind of kept herself to herself."

I consider his assessment of her. "God, it's so tragic."

Guy takes my hand and we continue on along the walk, an easy silence between us. He strokes my hand softly with his thumb.

Then out of the blue he muses, "You never really know the day or hour, do you?"

Guy had a habit of doing this. Throwing out a philosophical comment now and again. I suppose it was the writer in him.

"Yeah, I guess."

"I mean, one day you're moseying along, and everything is fine. The next, bam. All gone."

It was a depressing thought, but I guess he was right.

"That's why we're so lucky to have each other," he says, squeezing my hand a little tighter.

"Yeah," I agree.

We decide to stop off at our favourite Indian on the way home. I can't be bothered to cook and neither can Guy. But we don't exactly want to call it a night and sit in all evening either. So we decide on the Bengal Brasserie on the Lisburn Road.

Sitting opposite each other in the candle-lit restaurant, we order our usual. Korma for me, Tikka Masala for him, poppadums and beers for both of us.

"Cheers!" I say, clinking bottles with him.

"To us," Guy says. "Kate," he asks, looking serious.

"What?" He's making me feel nervous. I hate it when he does this, as though he's going to announce something awful.

"We still love each other very much don't we?"

I look at him in surprise. "Of course we do, honey. What makes you ask that?"

Guy and I have been together for five years. Living together for three. Surely he has no need to question our love for each other.

He looks a bit embarrassed. "I dunno, it's just that…" He's fiddling with the label on the beer bottle. He's gently picking at the paper label and pulling it gently.

I place a hand gently on his hand, to subtly make him stop picking and look at me.

He takes a deep breath. "It's just that… you see stuff like today… stuff like Kyle and Hannah and… it makes you realise how lucky you are… how that… everything you need…. everything you want…. is right under your nose… and…"

He stops talking for a moment and takes a long swig of his beer. I keep my eyes on him, listening intently. Bless him. He gets himself so wound up sometimes. Such a worrier. I know that if I listen to him talk it out, whatever it is that's bothering him will pass.

"Marry me, Kate," he says finally. He says it so quickly I'm not actually sure I've heard him right.

"Marry me," he repeats. He puts one hand up, his palm facing outwards. "I know we discussed it ages ago and I know it wasn't the right timing, but Kate, it's the right timing now, isn't it? Surely a day like today shows us that. I mean, you're all I want. You're all I need and…" He's taking my hand and he's clasping it in mine.

"Korma?" the waitress trills loudly, picking the most inopportune moment to bring the food.

"Er, here," I say, taking my hand away from Guy and leaving space for the waitress to set down my plate.

"Oooooh-kay!" she sings loudly. "And you must be the Tikka!" she continues merrily, placing Guy's plate before him.

"Er, thanks," he mumbles quietly.

"I'll just bring the poppadums over!" she smiles. "Anything else I can get you?"

I shake my head. "No, that's it thanks."

She has broken the moment and Guy looks wounded, as though he's not sure where to look.

"Guy," I begin. But I can tell that my tone of voice has

already given me away. He looks defeated.

"Guy, you know we've discussed this before. You know how I feel about marriage."

"Poppadums," the cheery waitress says, setting the basket on the table and then trotting off, her ponytail swinging behind her.

I can hardly look at the disappointment on Guy's face.

"Guy," I say softly. "We don't need a certificate to tell people how much we love each other…. Why fix something if it isn't broken?"

Guy shakes his head quietly. "No, Kate. I don't want to hear those excuses again. If you really loved me, you wouldn't need to use those excuses."

I look at him, his petulant face like that of a little child. I can't help but feel a moment of indignation rise within me.

"That's not fair," I say. "And you know it." I take a sip of my beer and look at him. "You can't throw that 'you mustn't love me' card. You know how I feel about marriage. I would be like this with anyone. I told you this before. So many times." I take another gulp of my beer for good measure. Maybe the froth will dampen down the bubbling emotion inside of me. Why did he have to spoil a perfectly good day? Why did he have to start this marriage thing again?

"I just think," he says slowly, as though picking his words carefully. "If you were with a man that you really love, you'd forget about all your commitment issues and you'd just go for it."

I roll my eyes. I can't help it. I'm glad the restaurant is quiet because I feel an argument bubbling up between us and I'm not going to back down.

"Oh really. Do you?" I say, a hint of sarcasm in my voice. "So, even after all the shit I watched between my parents, even after all the marriages I've seen break down, you think that some magical Adonis is going to saunter into my life and change all my lifelong views on marriage then, do you?"

I want a cigarette now. I want the deep inhalation of nicotine to course through my veins and calm my beating heart. I hate it when he gets like this. Whiny, insecure, claustrophobic. For god's sake! I'd hardly be with him for five years if I didn't love him. I'd hardly be letting him stay in my house rent free if I didn't want him kicking around.

"This is what this is about, isn't it?" I ask suddenly, a light-bulb moment going off in my head. "Is this about the house thing? Are you wanting your name on the mortgage or something?"

The minute the words are out of my mouth, I could kick myself. He looks horrified. And worse than that, he looks hurt. I've just managed to emasculate him in one fell swoop, five minutes after he's proposed to me. Nice work, Kate.

"Guy, I'm sorry, I shouldn't have said that," I say immediately, reaching a hand over to touch his. But he pulls it away quickly.

"Well, you've made your feelings quite clear," he says.

I could cry. The look of pain on his face is unbearable. I just want to give him a big hug and make it all better.

"I need a cigarette," he says, jumping up and storming off.

I sit there, in limbo, not sure what to do. Our food waits, uneaten, steam piping from it.

Ponytail waitress saunters past, a big grin on her face.

"Er… could I get these in a doggy bag? We're going to leave."

"Oh, okay!" she replies, at least having the good grace to look discreet. "No problem, I'll do that right now."

Within several minutes I've paid for the bill and I'm heading outside with the food in tubs.

I find him sitting at the restaurant patio table outside, smoking a cigarette.

I sit down next to him, not saying anything, and pull out a cigarette of my own.

"I do love you, you know, Guy." I say, quietly. "I do want to be with you for all time. I just…" I trail off. How can I explain it? How can I explain that I don't want to be a carbon copy of my parents? How can I explain that I promised myself that I'd never end up as trapped as my mum would be? How can I explain that the idea of commitment makes me feel like I can't breathe?

"But what you said just then," Guy says, his voice low. "You think I'm some sort of free-loading waster... that I'm just..."

"No! No I don't!" I persist. "I really don't Guy. I know what our set-up is. I know about your writing. I know how important it is to you. And I have faith in you, I really do!"

"So why have you just made me feel like shit on your shoe?"

I feel so frustrated. How many times do I have to reassure him that I love him? If he can't believe it himself, then how can I convince him?

He stands up and starts to walk away.

"Where are you going?" I ask.

"Home," he says. And then I hear him give a derisory chuckle. As though home was the most ironic place that he could call it.

I feel my heart shatter into a million pieces. Tonight, my boyfriend asked to marry me. Tonight I threw it right back in his face.

Chapter Twelve

Kerry

"Time for a quick cuppa while Barry gets the warrant?" I ask Simon.

"Defo," he replies, climbing the stairs with me back to our office.

We swing by the communal coffee dock which is en-route. Mercifully it's empty. I can deal with male police banter ninety percent of the time, but today I'm feeling a little fragile. Last night I was on a date and though I only had a few glasses of wine, I'm still feeling a little tender. Of course I'm not going to admit that to Simon. It wouldn't look good for my desire to climb the career ladder if he knows I'm hungover.

Simon sits at one of the tables and pulls out his phone. Gesturing in a jokey manner to me, he says, "A coffee would be great."

I give him a mock accusatory salute.

"Oh," I say. "Is it 'cos I'm the woman that I have the joy of making the coffee?"

I pick up the tea towel that's lying on the counter, twirl it in my hands, and playfully swipe at him. Just at that moment Barry arrives.

"Aye, aye," Barry chirps up in his thick Belfast accent. "Don't let me disturb the flirtation."

I immediately feel my cheeks redden. Thankfully my short spell of working at the police has already enabled me to deal with the banter. The best thing to do is banter straight back and pretend like it doesn't bother me.

"Barry," I say in my best patronising voice. "This eejit

thinks that just because I'm a woman, I should be running around making the tea for him. I'm not sure if he's just popped out of the fifties or what!"

"Actually," Simon chips in, "You're making the tea cos I made it the last time and you never get up off your arse to put the kettle on."

My mouth opens in disdain, but I move towards the kettle anyway as the three of us then lapse into chat about the Hannah case.

"Pete will be looking up further records on him later." Barry says. "I wonder if we find a history of domestic violence or something."

I feel my stomach squeeze at the thought of it. Domestic violence cases are a little triggering for me, but I don't like to admit it. It's not exactly professional to appear flaky and terrified. One of these days I'll learn to switch off and feel no emotion whatsoever.

"You think?" I ask.

"Well, it's pretty obvious," Simon answers. "Most of the time, a lot of suspects are much closer to home than we'd imagine. The public will assume it's some random rapist, but the motive is usually linked to someone who's very close."

I can feel goose-bumps at the thought of it. Could Kyle be our suspect all along?

We gulp back our tea in record time and discuss the case to prep each other before the visit. Then we're off and heading towards our cars.

A low ringtone erupts from Simon's pocket. He pulls the phone out of his pocket and hits the answer button.

"Hey there," he says, his voice immediately dropping to a softer tone.

It must be his wife Laura on the other end. She's the only person he reserves that tone of voice for.

I notice a brief feeling of longing in my chest. Imagine if someone reserved that soft tone for me. I quickly swipe that idea away. Jeez, what age am I, fourteen? I'm about to go out on a potential domestic abuse case for god's sake, now is not the time for fantasising like some rom-com character.

"Yeah," Simon says, continuing in his soft voice. "I should be home at normal time tonight. Why don't we go out for dinner for a change?"

Bastards, I think. I imagine my own measly microwave dinner for one, on a tray on my lap, watching reality TV. Meanwhile, Simon, Laura and their two beautiful children, will be sitting around some fancy table in some swanky restaurant, eating some exquisite cuisine. There will probably be a piano tinkering away in the background. Well-dressed waiters in bow ties and big smiles will be attending to their every whim.

Simon wraps the call up with Laura. I can tell that she must have told him she loved him because he responds with, "Yeah, me too."

I glance over at him while he puts his phone back in his pocket.

Jokingly, I say, "Oh you think you'll be done by six, do you? You're optimistic!"

My tone is jokey, but his grimace is serious. "Jeez, don't be saying that," he says. "If I'm not home on time tonight, my guts will be for garters."

I give him a quizzical look.

"Caitlin's birthday," he says.

"Ahhh," I nod. "So you have to be there or…"

Simon quickly finishes my sentence, "… or Laura would probably divorce me."

"Don't exaggerate," I say.

"Trust me," he says, as we career down the back steps and out towards the car. "It's a thin line."

Just at that moment another officer walks past and stops Simon briefly for a quick chat about some other case. But Simon's words are still ringing in my ears. A thin line towards divorce? Surely not? They seemed like the world's perfect couple.

But then again, what do I know? The longer I'm in this job, the more dodgy domestic situations I see and the less my romantic fairy-tale ending seems possible.

But I still can't get over Simon's admission about the

57

potential divorce. Surely he's joking. I've seen the photo of Laura and the kids. It's pride of place on his desk. It's one of those picture-perfect moments. They're all grinning. His daughter has his arms wrapped tightly around his neck. They all look like they're glowing with ecstatic joy.

"It's this job that's a killer," Simon says as we're in his car and driving towards Kyle's house. "If you've just caught a criminal and you want to do a two-hour interrogation on him, you can't suddenly say to him, 'oh hold that thought mister, I just need to go home and check on the kids and the missus.' The job comes first unfortunately."

I muse over this thought as I glance at him driving. He's concentrating intently on the road, and I can't help looking at his hands, gripping the steering wheel, his left hand reaching down to the gearstick, the light bouncing off the wedding ring on his finger.

Something shifts in me and I'm not sure what it is. Is it the realisation that Simon and I would be more suited, that we spend so much time together anyway? Or am I just throwing about stupid ideas in my head?

Simon glances over at me. "You're lucky," he says.

I gulp. "Me? Lucky? Why?"

"Well you're young, free and single. You can come and go as you please. You don't have to answer to anyone. You're not disappointing anyone…" he trails off.

"Yeah, and I'm not shagging anyone." I've put on a jokey tone, although I suddenly feel embarrassed about being so personal.

Simon raises an eyebrow. "I'm sure you could have a different guy every night of the week."

I gulp. Jesus. Is he flirting with me? "Hmmph!" I grimace. "I wish!"

There's an awkward silence then and, because I can't bear a silence, I pipe up. "Well actually, I was on a date last night."

Simon chuckles. "Oh! Here we go, what did I say?"

I chuckle back.

"Well," he probes. "You can't stop there. Come on, spill.

What was he like?"

I groan. "Oh, do I have to tell you?"

"Yes," he says. "I can give you good tips about men. After all, I am one."

"You don't say," I jest. "I thought you were some sort of weird alien from another planet."

"Stop stalling, Ker. Come on, spill. What was he like?" Simon probes.

"Okay, well… I met him in the House bar last night, in Stranmillis," I begin.

"Internet date?" he interrupts.

"How the flip did you know that?" I ask.

"Everyone's doing it these days," Simon shrugs.

"So we meet. He seems nice enough," I continue. "Tall, attractive, slim."

"Tall, attractive, slim," Simon repeats. "That's your type, okay."

"And he offers me a drink, and we sit and chat. And you know, we get on okay. The chat is easy enough. He can hold a conversation."

"Good, good," Simon agrees. "Has teeth, has hair, can talk."

"But…"

"There's a but?"

"But, and this is gonna sound bad. He doesn't pay for the drinks."

"Huh?"

"Well he pays for the first round, and then I offer to pay for the next one, and he lets me. And then he pays the next round and then he allows me to pay for the next round."

Simon looks at me confused. "And this is a problem, why?"

"Well, it's the first date. I mean, jeez, if he can't treat you on the first date, well, it's all downhill from here on isn't it?"

Simon shakes his head. "You women, seriously."

"What?"

"Well if he holds the door open you feel like it's offensive. If he doesn't hold the door, you feel it's rude. You want to be treated equally and be all girl power, but then you want him to buy all the rounds…"

"I know but…" I say defensively. "It was the first date. You'd think he'd make an effort on the first date."

Simon gives me a knowing look. "All I'm saying is that the next time we stop for a coffee, remind me to pay for it. I don't want the Cash Police after me."

I playfully hit him across the arm. "Another thing," I add. "At the end of the night, I was really starving. I wanted to go for a dirty great burger. But he was all 'my body's a temple. I'll wait until I go home to cook some eggs and quinoa.'"

"Oh, fuck that," Simon agrees.

"I know."

"I mean, if you can't have a good couples takeaway feast together, then where's the fun in that?"

"Exactly."

"Did he snog you?" Simon asked.

It never fails to amaze me how direct Simon is. The questions just roll off his tongue with the same directness he uses on suspects.

"Er… yeah," I admit.

"Any good?"

"It was okay."

"Just okay?" Simon grunts. "Just okay on a first date is pretty crap."

There's a moment of comfortable silence and then Simon pipes up with, "I think you're just not the marrying type."

"Huh?"

"Yeah, you just strike me as one of those independent girls. Who would rather live on her own and do her own thing."

I mull this over, wondering if this is the case. I'd always thought I'd want the happy ever after. The husband, the 2.4 kids, the white picket fence. But then I think back to previous boyfriends. Their mess. Their piss on the bathroom floor. Their pubes scattered over the shower. Their shoes dragging in dirty marks on the carpet. There was something exquisite about living on my own. About having the place to myself.

About having it tidy and cute and girlie. About having the control of the remote. Maybe Simon was right.

"It's not all it's cracked up to be, you know," Simon says, interrupting my thoughts.

"It's not?"

"No way. All the sleepless nights. All your money disappearing as though someone's chucked it down the drain. And don't get me started on the worry. They get sick; you worry. They have to go to the doctors; you worry. They need dental treatment; you worry. I'm already worrying about Caitlin turning sixteen. Can you imagine when blokes start dating her?"

"I feel very sorry for the blokes indeed," I joke. "You'll be hauling them in for questioning and I'm pretty sure they'll be running a mile in the other direction away from her."

"Good. That would be my intention."

I chuckle.

"And don't get me started on the guilt. They get sick; you feel guilty. You tell yourself that you brought them into this world; you've caused the pain."

"Ouch, that's a bit harsh."

"Seriously though," he says. "Enjoy it while it lasts."

Chapter Thirteen

Hannah

"Who's this guy named Guy?"

I noticed Kyle's tone of voice before I even looked up and saw the sneer plastered all over his face.

He was holding my mobile phone, looking at me with all the interrogation of a top-grade detective.

"What are you doing going through my phone?" The words were out of my mouth before I even had time to think about them. I should have known that that kind of response would have only made him angrier.

He raised his eyebrows and sneered further. "Oh, so you *do* have something to hide, do you?"

He crossed the room towards me, an anger in his step which made my shoulders hunch up and my body curve inwards away from him.

He saw my physical reaction and gave me a snide look. "What do you think I'm gonna do to you huh?" His words were forceful, the spit from his mouth landing on my cheeks, making me blink away in disgust.

"Would this scare you, huh?"

Then his hands were up around my throat, not exactly grabbing it, but threatening to do so.

"Kyle! No! Please!" I snivelled, my voice sounding pathetic and weak in his grip.

"No! Please!" he mimicked back. "Tell me what you did with him!"

"I didn't do anything! Please!" I breathed. "He's just a friend from work!" My voice was raspy, each word coming out in short, scared bursts.

"Oh, he's just a friend is he?" Kyle pronounced each word with aggression, though his hand had moved away from my throat. Now his hand was scrolling through my phone messages.

"Hey Hannah," he read out, mimicking Guy's supposed flirtatious voice. "I was just thinking about you and wondering if you're okay. Let me know if you ever want a coffee and a chat." He spat out the ending, "Kiss."

I held my breath, not knowing what to say. And then I feebly managed, "You see, he's just a friend."

Guy forced out a strangled laugh. "Oh you pathetic naïve little girl, Hannah. When blokes say coffee, they mean sex."

"No…" I gasped, but his hand was back at my throat again.

"If you go anywhere near this Guy twat, I swear I …." His hand gripped around my neck and I gasped, but he quickly loosened his grip again. He chucked the phone on the bed and stormed out of the bedroom, slamming the door behind him.

I fell to the bed, my breathing quick and panicky. I couldn't think straight. My thoughts were swimming in my head. I couldn't believe that just happened. Did he really just threaten to strangle me?

I heard the front door slam shut and his car start up in the driveway. He'd gone, thank god.

I sat there on the bed for I don't know how long. I guess I must've been in shock because I couldn't move. I couldn't believe what had just happened.

***

The following day at work Guy asked me if I got his text.

"Oh yeah, sorry," I murmured. "I forgot to reply."

I tried to ignore the hurt expression that crossed his face. I told myself that I had enough to worry about never mind trying to please people at work.

On the other hand, perhaps this was my opportunity. I should sit Guy down and I should tell him what Kyle did. I should ask for Guy's help. Where do I go from here? How do I run away from Kyle? How would I start afresh?

But I was still in a bubble of shock and denial. I couldn't think straight; never mind wondering how I was going to escape.

So instead, I did what any other (in)sane woman would do.

I blocked Guy's number so Kyle would find no further messages.

I went to the doctor and asked for strong sleeping pills and heavy sedatives.

And I went to the off-licence and bought several bottles of vodka.

Bottle number one; I hid at the bottom of my underwear drawer.

Bottle number two; I hid in the hot-press behind all the towels.

And bottle number three; I hid at the bottom of the laundry basket underneath a towel.

I went home from work, knocked back my tablets, swigged them back with a stiff drink, and entered the land of not giving a fuck.

Kyle could be as nuts as he wanted. I was in cloud zombie-land; I no longer cared.

When he was in a stinking mood and he decided to take it out on me, I was past caring because I'd be zonked.

Like the time he couldn't get the orange juice out of the Tupperware jug. So he huffed and puffed and finally got the god-damn lid off the jug and then threw the lid across the room. I don't think I even flinched.

I started to realise that two could play at this game. If he wanted to act like an asshole and not live up to the vows he made on our wedding day, I could too.

When I went to do our weekly food-shop, I paid for it with a cheque from our joint account.

"Oh, excuse me love," I said to the girl behind the till. "Could you round that up to an extra thirty quid and just give me the cashback?"

"Of course!" she helpfully obliged. She pressed the three

clean, fresh notes in my hand and I felt a joyous feeling of "fuck you" wash over me.

"Fuck you Kyle. Two can play at this game."

But then other times he would act all lovey-dovey, as though everything was grand, and he had never held a hand to my throat to threaten to strangle me.

He would take me out for dinner and we would sit in a fancy restaurant, and a candle would be flickering in between us. I would catch the eye of other restaurant goers and I could almost imagine the thoughts that would go through their heads. 'Look at that perfect couple, they look like they have the idyllic life'. If only they knew.

Kyle would take me home and he would be that same, loving, charming man that I had first fallen in love with. And if I could forget the recent events, it was almost as if I was in a time-warp. But of course I couldn't forget. Not unless I knocked back some vodka on the quiet. Vodka that trickled down to my toes and made me warm and woozy and made me not care.

It made me not care that Kyle was sidling up to me on the sofa and whispering sweet nothings into my ear, his breath hot and clammy on my skin. Vodka helped me resist the urge to shove him off me. Vodka helped me to let him kiss me, his tongue plunging into my mouth and searching my tongue out. Vodka helped me to allow him to pull my top up and pull down my bra and let his tongue swirl all over my nipple. Vodka helped me not to mind when he pulled down his trousers and pushed himself inside me, coming heavily and gasping loud into my ear.

And when it was over, when he had fallen asleep, I'd lie there and make plans. Plans to get away. Plans to tell someone. Plans to escape.

I thought my plans through. What if I told Guy? What could he do? Being a listening ear was one thing. But what could he do? He couldn't lift me out of my home and plant me in a new home where Kyle would never find me. And anyway, it was too big an ask. Being a sympathetic colleague with a listening ear was one thing. Helping someone move into a new home was another.

What if I went to a women's refuge? They would say, "Does he hit you?" And I would say, "Well no, but he did hold his hand to my throat once, but he didn't actually do anything." They would shake their head sorry and say that I wasn't a serious case.

What if I tried to find a flat of my own? But he would hunt me down and find me and he wouldn't let me go.

So I lay there, in the middle of the night, making endless plans to escape but each plan seemed to have a massive loophole.

It got to the point where I stopped caring, where one comment went in one ear and out the other.

Like the time I had dressed up to go for dinner with him. I thought he'd approve of my red dress; its plunging neckline, my hair piled on top of my hair with tendrils softly cascading down the sides. But he took one look at me and said, "Are you wearing that?"

I looked down at myself. "Er, yeah. Don't you like it?"

He shrugged. "Bit tarty hun, no?"

He saw my hurt expression and crossed the room towards me. I shied away from him like a scared puppy, but he planted a kiss on my forehead. "You'd look good in anything hun," he purred. "But you don't need all this make-up and this…." His finger drifted down towards my cleavage. "It's not you."

I knew what the hidden subtext was. "Don't wear make-up and don't wear slutty clothes."

So from then on I wore only a hint of make-up. A little foundation, a little cover-up, that was it.

I wore sedate dresses in navy blue and black. Dresses that fell below the knee and covered up above the chest. Dresses that made me feel anonymous, like I was melting into the background. Dresses that turned no head and raised no eyebrow.

But my planning continued. My parallel universe. I told myself that one day I would be free of him. One day I would prance around in short skirts and full make-up. I would look like a ridiculous clown if I wanted to, and it wouldn't matter what anyone thought.

Meanwhile he seemed to take even more pride in his appearance. He wore expensive designer suits with flashy cufflinks. He had found some 'amazing' fancy barber that cut his hair using fresh blades; a visit which apparently cost him one hundred pounds. He looked like something out of a GQ magazine. Polished to within every inch of his life.

I'm sure other people looked at us. I'm sure they said to themselves, "What is he doing with her? He's so handsome and she's so …. well, dowdy."

I wonder if that's what he wanted. That air of being in charge. The one in control. The one with the power.

I wasn't stupid, I could see his wandering eye. I could see the way his eyes would linger over the waitress. The way he would smile at her, as though she was the only girl in the room. I could see the way she sparkled under his gaze, as though a spotlight had been shone upon her. I wouldn't be one bit surprised if he left his phone number for her on the table after we left. I wouldn't be one bit surprised if he was fucking her the very next night.

In some ways I wished he would. I wished she'd take him off my hands for me.

But I wasn't stupid. I knew what my role had become. I was the cook, the cleaner, the reliable shag. All the other girls were exciting sexy time.

And then something happened that made me not able to leave. The day that I saw the two blues lines on the tiny stick. The day that I realised I was pregnant.

Now there was no going back. Now I was stuck with him. Now he was the father of my child.

I should have been overjoyed. Correction, I was overjoyed. All along, that was all I had ever wanted. A baby to love, who would love me back. That unconditional bond.

I swore to that unborn baby that I would do everything to love and care for and protect this little bundle of growth inside of me.

Kyle was overjoyed too of course. He hugged me tightly

and even had tears in his eyes. "We did it!" he exclaimed with utter joy as he looked at the two lines of confirmation in shock. "We did it!"

I nodded, smiling too. It was one of those pure, blissful, happy moments. One of those moments that stand still. One of those moments where you forget everything that went before, when you don't fret about what's ahead. When you just glow in the absolute joy of right here.

And you wish that it could stay like that forever.

Chapter Fourteen

Julia & Kyle

"Shall we go upstairs?" Kyle whispers, as his hand reaches my leg and creeps upwards, underneath my skirt.

"Yes!" a voice inside me whispers. The voice that has been single forever. The voice that can't remember the last time a man was kissing me like this, wanting me.

But the outer voice, the physical voice, somehow comes out with the words, "Are you sure?"

He draws back from me and I could instantly kick myself. What am I saying? Why am I trying to put him off?

He looks at me, his face a mixture of embarrassment and confusion. "I'm sorry…" he says. "I thought this was what you wanted…."

I take his hand immediately and try to placate him. "I do!" I soothe. "Of course I do… It's just that…." I trail off, unsure of how to word this without hurting his feelings.

I'm aware, all the while, that any tingle of desire he might have had for me is probably fading fast.

No wonder I'm single! I reprimand myself. A quick Filofax flickers through my mind as I remind myself that all my friends are currently loved up and I'm the only sad singleton left among us. Now, here on my very sofa, a man is offering me love and affection, and I'm throwing it back in his face! I should be lapping it up, enjoying the attention.

"I guess I'm just thinking about Hannah. I mean…"

Kyle shifts in his seat.

"I suppose I feel I'm being disrespectful to Hannah, and I'm aware your head must be all over the place."

"No, you're right," he leans up to touch my face. "I knew there was something different about you, Julia. Something special. You've got a good heart."

I feel my insides tingle in appreciation.

His hand traces from my cheek down towards my lips. His finger traces lightly over my lip and I feel the sensation trickle down to my groin. My body is screaming for him.

"I suppose I just can't help myself," he whispers. "There's something about you. I just feel drawn to you…"

And with that he's leaning over, and his lips are on mine, and his tongue is searching mine out passionately. I can't help it. I'm lost. All thought and reasoning has gone out the window. And this time I'm not going to argue. I'm not going to overthink it. I'm just going to go with it.

He places one hand under my knees and scoops me up effortlessly. I giggle as he carries me up the stairs. Then he sets me down briefly, to kiss me on the stairs, his hand reaching to the inside of my thighs, his fingers tracing over me. Then, as though he can't wait any longer, he picks me up again, carries me to my room, throws me lightly on the bed and quickly peels off my clothes.

***

We must have fallen into a slumber afterwards because when I wake I can see the sunlight trying to poke through the curtains. I look over at him and see him lying there, fast asleep. I can't help it. I just stare at him for a while, savouring him, drinking him in. The way that his mouth hangs open slightly, the way that his hair is tousled over his forehead. I then look over at the alarm clock. It reads 7:18. I could just lie here and stare at him for a while, but if he wakes and catches me doing that it would be super awkward. I decide instead to pad into the bathroom and freshen myself up a little. I wash my face, slap on some moisturiser, brush my teeth and brush my hair. Then I decide on the smallest amount of make-up, enough for me to have a fresh glow look about me, rather than one of too much effort.

I head downstairs and put on a fresh brew of coffee so that the filtered aroma will fill the house and create a welcoming vibe when he wakes.

I even go the full works and stick on a few rashers of bacon. Surely the scent of freshly cooked bacon is the way to any man's heart.

Sitting at the dining room table, coffee in one hand, magazine in the other, I hear his footsteps creak down the stairs.

"Hey!" I smile as he enters the room.

He nods formally. "Hey."

I can tell immediately that he hasn't woken up yet. His eyes seem bleary and he looks disorientated.

"Coffee?" I ask, jumping up from my chair to hurry to the kitchen.

"Er... sorry, no. I really better dash on."

"Oh, okay…" I try to hide my disappointment. "I have bacon…" I add, limply..

He looks at his watch. "I'm really sorry. I need to dash. I have an early meeting today…"

"It's no problem!"

He grabs his shoes from the rug, a nod to where they had been kicked off last night in a more relaxed vibe. Shoving his feet into them and picking up his coat from the edge of the chair he adds, "Well, thanks again. I'll be in touch."

I try to ignore the feelings of humiliation that are running through me. I can tell a shag-and-run when I see it. And this is clearly a shag-and-run.

"Bye then," he says, a quick peck on my cheek, and then he's gone, the door slamming behind him.

The noise makes me close my eyes momentarily, a wave of self-disgust pouring over me.

I know what that was. A pity shag. A grieving shag. A sympathy shag.

No wonder he's feeling guilty. His wife is missing, probably hidden in some rapist's den, and meanwhile he's off shagging around.

I sigh, pacing around my apartment as I try to busy myself. I tidy the coffee cups into the kitchen, lift the plate of uneaten bacon and tip it into the bin. I put the crockery into the basin of hot soapy water as though washing away last night's evidence will erase the memory of what happened.

How could I be so stupid? How could I have fallen for all his charm? When am I ever going to learn to hold out for a while before I shag a guy? I'm still pacing back and forth, my mind whirling in self-disgust. I'm like a caged animal.

I spy my trainers in the corner of my room and decide the best thing to do is to go for a run to try to work off this tension. Returning from the run I'm invigorated. I've made a plan. Kyle is no more. I will not reply to any of his messages. I won't see him again. My days of being treated like a mug are over. That's it, Mister Kyle! I will not be helping you in your campaign anymore!

***

A few days pass and there's no word from Kyle. I'm relieved and disgusted in equal measures. At least I don't have to see him again or make excuses not to see him again. But then Friday night arrives, and I receive what can only be a drunken text. It's past midnight when my phone bleeps.

It simply reads:
Hey Julia x
I look at the screen and then throw the phone back down on the sofa in disgust. I'm not answering that.

I have my comfort blanket over me, a glass of red wine in one hand, and the remote control in the other. I've been drinking since seven pm and I'm rightly on. But no matter how pissed I am, I'm not replying to him.

The phone bleeps again.
Are you awake? X
I roll my eyes. *Yes, I'm awake, you plonker. But that doesn't mean I want to reply to you.*

Another bleep. This text is a longer one. In fact, it's practically a novel.

I'm so sorry about the other day, Julia. I know I disappeared really quickly, but I was really ashamed of myself. I know it was wrong what I did, and I felt so guilty about Hannah. But I really like you Julia. I like you a lot. That's the problem I guess, I feel so guilty, but I know there is a connection between us. I'd love to talk to you about this in person Julia. Please can we talk? Xx

I still don't reply but I do notice a hint of a smile cross my lips. I can feel myself melting. Kyle is like sitting next to a hot fire, you can't help but feel yourself defrost next to his flames.

But I still don't reply. I think I'll let him stew for a while longer.

The phone bleeps again.

Okay, I respect your wishes. Goodbye Julia, and thanks for everything xx

I roll my eyes. Jeez, what a drama queen. Just because I'm not jumping to his messages, he's doing the goodbye flouncing thing.

And yet, somehow, my fingers find themselves floating over the keypad and typing a quick response. As though they're magically moving at their own accord.

I was really hurt by the way you disappeared off. I type.

Immediately my phone comes to life with a ringing tone and accompanying flashing light. I see his name bleep on the screen. Kyle is calling.

My fingers hit the answer button and my voice says, "Hello?" in a soft, quiet tone.

"Julia," he says. His voice sounds breathy, grateful, happy to hear me.

"Kyle," I respond, my tone still huffy and formal.

"Julia, please, can I come round? I really want to talk to you."

I look at the clock. 12:15. "It's the middle of the night! What do you want to come around now for?"

"I can jump in a cab. I'll be there in twenty. I'll bring some wine. Please Julia, I really want to talk to you."

There's a silence then, as I'm digesting this. I'd need to get dressed. I'd need to put my make-up on. I don't have work tomorrow though so at least I could sleep in.

"Okay…." I agree begrudgingly.

"Okay! See you soon!" he says breathily, and then he's hanging up, before I can change my mind.

Bollocks, I say, and I set the phone down. I jump up, rushing upstairs to get dressed and tidy myself up. Just as I'm applying a bit of lippy and shooshing my hair into a bed head tousled look, the doorbell rings.

I head downstairs, taking my time. Why I think I'm playing it cool after accepting a late-night call I don't know. But I open the door slowly and look at him standing there.

He is smiling, with a bottle in either hand. "Red or white? One of each?" he grins.

I smile, unable to resist his cheeky grin. "Come in," I say warily, with the voice an over-tired mother would use with their child.

It's only when we're sitting cross-legged on the floor, leaning against the sofa that he starts to talk about Hannah. We each have a glass of wine and Kyle has rolled a spliff which we're passing back and forth to each other.

"The police are really on my case," he confides, and he exhales smoke in my direction.

"Huh? On your case? Why?"

He shrugs his shoulders. "I dunno. They said it's something to do with thesuspect. Apparently the first suspect is always the one closest to the person. Apparently they always question the partner first."

"But that's ridiculous!" I exclaim. "You're her husband. You're the one who made the call. You're the one who's trying to find her."

He sighs. "I know. It's ridiculous. I don't understand it either. They're wasting precious time interrogating me when they could be out there looking for her killer."

"Do you really believe that? Do you think the person who took her is going to kill her?"

Kyle shifted a little. "Well, I don't know. I'm only surmising."

It's such an awkward topic.

I place a comforting hand on Kyle's arm. Maybe it's the wine that's relaxing me. Maybe it's the spliff. But suddenly

I'm annoyed at myself for being so huffy. Of course Kyle is going to be off with me and acting strange. His wife has gone missing. She's probably lying dead somewhere. Kyle is drinking the bit out and smoking his brains off to try to cope with it all. So he got a bit drunk and we had a bit of a drunken mistake. So what!

"I really hope you're not still mad at me," Kyle whispers, as though reading my mind. "I really don't want to hurt you. You're the best friend I've got at the moment. I feel like I can confide in you…"

"I'm glad you can confide in me," I whisper.

And then I let him hug me. I let him bury his head into my chest. I feel the closeness and warmth between us. I savour the moment. I forget about all the previous anxiety. I forget all about what could happen next. And I just enjoy the warmth and closeness of now. And somehow, his mouth reaches mine again. And somehow, we're kissing again.

Chapter Fifteen

Hannah

The initial excitement of the pregnancy wore off quickly for Kyle. Sure, there was that euphoria at first, that utter awe that his sperm had joined with my eggs. That deep down inside of me was a cluster of cells growing and forming into our little baby. But his excitement quickly waned. It was as if Kyle had a certain level of irritation in his cup, and every day that irritation had to spill out.

It reared its ugly head only a week or so later. I had dropped my guard, spurred on by Kyle's recent charm; the way that he had cuddled up to me; the way that he had cooed over my belly; the way that he chatted to the baby inside my tummy with that cute little voice he had used. I had stupidly believed that maybe this was the making of us. That maybe this baby would change everything. That maybe this was all he needed all along, to have that excitement of welcoming his mini-me into the world.

I woke up before him one Saturday morning and decided to go downstairs and bake some pancakes. I thought the aroma would fill the house with a comforting embrace. I look back at it now and think how stupid I was. How could a few pancakes change everything?

"Morning!" I'd said cheerily, when he finally arrived downstairs.

"Morning," he'd responded gruffly. "Why are you so happy?" He sat at the kitchen table, waiting for me to bring him his first coffee of the day.

"Oh, I don't know!" I replied in a sing-song voice. "It's a beautiful morning, the smell of the pancakes, our little cherub in my tummy."

He grunted. His mood had the ability to slice through the air like a sharp knife.

Immediately I inwardly recoiled. I knew what this mood meant. This mood meant sit down, shut up and act subservient. Perhaps that was it. Perhaps I'd gotten too big for my boots. Perhaps he'd spotted my cocky attitude and wanted to put me back in my place again. I was getting too confident.

I lifted the jug from the filter machine and poured the thick, black liquid into the cup. I knew the correct amount of milk to add. Too little and he'd complain. Too much and he'd complain. I had to measure it just right. I lifted the little carton of sweetener and squeezed the button four times. One, two, three, four, careful not to zap in too many. I took the cup over to him and set it down before him. I said nothing. Nor did he. No thank you. No small talk. Nothing.

I lifted a pancake from the plate in the middle of the table and set it on my own plate. My appetite had actually waned but it seemed like a waste not to eat the freshly prepared breakfast. Reaching for the maple syrup, I applied it heartily over the pancake. I caught his eye as he was watching me.

Finally he opened his mouth. "Are you gonna have some pancake with your syrup?"

It was his sarcastic way of telling me that I was too greedy. That there was no need to be applying so much syrup.

I tried to make light of it. "Well, I'm eating for two now!"

I thought he would have laughed and agreed. I thought that his early excitement for the baby would have jostled him out of this stinking morning mood.

He took a sip of his coffee and then assessed me with that blank, non-caring stare. "There's eating for two," he said. "And then there's eating for one adult and one tiny cluster of cells."

I gulped back. So that was the message. I was getting too fat, too quickly. I was using the pregnancy excuse to eat whatever I wanted. Pizza, Ben & Jerry's, pancakes laden with syrup.

I set my pancake back down on my plate then. My appetite had immediately vanished. I tried to hold back the tears that were threatening to spill out. Oh how I needed my tablets. But what could I do about my tablets now? I couldn't eat as many of them as I once did. Wouldn't it harm the baby? And I couldn't knock back the vodka either. I was screwed. I had to sit with stone cold sobriety, with nothing to ease the pain.

The tears leaked out. Large fat goblets squeezed out of my sockets and rolled down my cheeks.

Kyle spotted them and sighed. He rolled his eyes. "Oh god, so we're going to put on the waterworks are we?" He stood up, his chair scraping harshly against the tiled floor. "Well guess what?" he seethed. "The waterworks aren't gonna wash with me today."

He stormed out of the kitchen. I heard him lift his keys. I heard him slam the front door behind him. And he was gone.

I was glad. I breathed a sigh of relief and hoped he stayed away all bloody day. I hoped he went somewhere and got rip-roaring pissed. I hoped he got so pissed that he staggered along somewhere and fell. I hoped that when he fell, a car would magically drive in front of him and run him over.

I needed a drink. Just one little drink. Just one soothing little tumbler of warmth. Just to take the edge of things. Surely one wouldn't hurt. You hear about loads of women having just one glass of wine when they're pregnant.

I had to be quick though. Kyle could land back home again any moment.

I dashed to the laundry basket. My hand delved under the dirty clothes past his used boxers, underneath a wet towel. Scrambling around, I couldn't find the damn bottle. My heart jumped when I thought I heard something. Had he returned? Was that him climbing the stairs again? I crept over to the top of the stairs but there was nothing. My mind was clearly playing tricks on me. I retreated back to the laundry basket. Scooping my hand beneath the stinky wet clothes, I couldn't feel the familiar hard cold touch of the bottle. In frustration, I pulled the clothes out of the basket, tossing them on the floor, searching for the bloody bottle. Nothing. There was no bottle there. What had I done with it? I'm sure I hadn't drunk it all. I'm sure there was some left. Could I really have finished that entire bottle?

"Looking for something?" his dark, angry voice made me jump.

I looked up to see him standing there, his dark figure silhouetted in the door frame.

"Kyle!" I exclaimed. "You made me jump!"

A faux-amused expression crossed his lips as he leaned against the doorway.

"Oh, I'm sorry," his voice was thick with sarcasm. "Did I interrupt you? Just what are you doing anyway?"

I know how it would have looked. There was me, on my knees, sitting on our plush carpet, next to our expensive bed, in our exquisitely designed bedroom, surrounded by a pile of dirty wet knickers.

"I'm just doing the laundry!" I replied, trying to keep a light tone in my voice.

"Just doing the laundry," he repeated, his voice thick with condescension. "Just doing the laundry." He crossed the room and sat on the bed, facing me.

I could feel my body shy away from him, as though instinctively protecting myself from attack. *Although, surely he wouldn't do anything to me now. Surely he wouldn't attack me now the baby is inside me.*

"You mean you're trying to find your bloody vodka!" his voice boomed with anger.

My heart hammered inside my chest. *How the fuck does he know that?*

"Drinking bloody vodka when our baby is inside you! How fucking selfish can you be?"

He reached over and grabbed my wrist, wrenching it with both hands. "How could you?"

I could see the veins in his neck standing on end; his jaw clenched. And the grip on my arm was getting tighter and tighter.

"Kyle! Please! Don't!" I squirmed, trying to wriggle away from him.

He dropped his hands suddenly, as though disgusted by my very presence. "How could you?" he asked. "How could you?"

The tears came rapidly then. I didn't even care anymore. I couldn't help it. I was crying non-stop, wondering how on earth my life had come to this. And this time I knew it was my fault. I knew I was the one in the wrong. I knew that it was me harming my baby.

He walked away to the door and turned back. Looking over his shoulder and down at me with disgust, he spat, "You need help."

What did he mean 'need help'? Did he mean one of those rooms with a semicircle of old men sitting around in trench coats, a bottle of whisky hidden in each pocket?

"You're mad, Hannah. You have a major problem. I've arranged for you to see a psychiatrist. You need to get this shit sorted. I will not have the mother of my child drinking the bit out during pregnancy."

He stormed off, his footsteps angrily marking each step on the way downstairs. "And don't even think about looking for any more of your stash!" he shouted. "I've found them all!"

My mind was racing as I looked down and noticed my trembling fingers. *How the fuck did he find out about my stash?* I thought I had hidden them so perfectly? When has he ever, ever, done the laundry in his entire life? How on earth did he come across that?

My fingers continued to shake as I leaned against the wall and tried to soothe the shaky feeling that was coursing through my entire body.

I wondered if he had installed secret cameras around the house and that was why he knew what I'd been up to.

But then I caught myself in my line of thinking. Jeez, I really did sound mad. Mad and paranoid. As if he'd go to the bother of installing secret cameras. And anyway, when would he have had the chance to install them when I was always there?

My hands dropped down to my tummy and I cradled my baby, apologising profusely. How could I do this to him?

How could I threaten his livelihood? Kyle was right, I was a bad mummy. A sick mummy. I needed help.

Maybe Kyle was right all along, and it was me with the problems?

I continued to rub my tummy, promising to my baby that I would do everything I possibly could to love and protect him, till death do us part.

***

The counsellor's room was tiny and basic. It was nothing like those fancy scenes you see on TV. There was a box of tissues, yes. And there were two chairs and one tiny table. But that was it; basic and plain. It looked more like a police interrogation room than some plush rehab facility.

"Now, Mrs Greer," the counsellor smiled kindly. "Maybe you could start by just telling me a little about yourself, about why you want this treatment?"

Spectacles rested on her nose. She was wearing a cosy jumper and a pair of black trousers. She had a mumsy look about her, as though she liked to bake cookies and make jam in her spare time.

"Hmm, well, actually it's my husband that suggested it," I said, squirming. I was full of anxiety. I was wondering if this was all some decoy. If she wasn't really a counsellor. Maybe she was a social worker pretending to be a counsellor. Maybe, if I confided about the pills and the drink, she'd take that as proof that I wouldn't be a fit mother. Maybe the minute my baby was born someone official looking would arrive in a dark suit and take my baby away.

Or maybe if I confided my fantasies about wanting Kyle to get so drunk that he fell and someone drove over him she would take it the wrong way. She may think I was planning to be the one to drive over him. Or she may think that I'd pay someone to do it for me.

"Mrs Greer…?" she asked, trying to distract me out of my reverie.

"Huh?"

"Mrs Greer..." she repeated, softly. "May I call you Hannah?"

She did look nice, really she did. She seemed kind and sweet and caring, but I knew what was going on here. I knew that she wanted to call me by my first name so that I would feel closer to her. She wanted things to be more intimate so that I opened up to her. But I wasn't stupid. I knew Kyle was behind all of this. There was probably a recording device tucked in behind those tissues.

"Can I take a tissue?" I asked, leaning over quickly before she could say no. I lifted the box and realised that there was no recording device hidden behind it. Maybe the recording device was somewhere else.

The counsellor was looking at me with a mixture of interest and confusion.

"Is there something on your mind?" she asked softly.

Something on my mind. Something on my mind. Oh yes, there was plenty on my mind. Plenty.

I shook my head, no.

"Hannah...I'm here to help you." Her voice was soothing, too soothing. I guessed this was what happened when they tried to interrogate you. They tried to soothe you into submission.

"I'm fine."

Counsellor's face crippled in confusion. I bet she was gutted she had to deal with me. I bet she was wishing she got a talker. Not a clammer-upper.

"Okay," she smiled. And then she sat there, quietly. I knew this technique. This was how they make you talk. Eventually you wouldn't be able to bear the silence and you'd pipe up and say something.

But I didn't. I just sat there. I watched the clock on the wall as the hand ticked by. Tick tock, tick tock.

I looked at the counsellor's face which was full of worry and pity.

I looked around the room wondering where the hidden recording equipment was.

I looked back at the clock. Tick tock, tick tock.

It became quite meditative actually. I was starting to enjoy it. One whole hour of nothing. One whole hour where I wouldn't be criticised. One whole hour where I wouldn't have to watch what I said or walk on egg-shells or tip-toe around the house.

One whole hour where I wouldn't have to jump if I heard the sound of his wheels crunch down the driveway. One whole hour. Tick, tock, tick, tock.

Chapter Sixteen

Hannah

"Hannah…" Counsellor lady said quietly, when we got to the fifty-minute mark. "Is there anything I can do to help you? Anything I can do to ease your mind?"

I looked at her, the cosy jumper, the glasses supported by their granny string. She was mumsy incarnate.

Oh, he chose well, I thought. He found someone cosy and safe looking and warm. She was someone he thought I would open up to, someone he thought I would confide in.

I remained tight-lipped.

"Hannah…." she said in that soft voice. "Call me Angela by the way."

My heart skipped a beat. Angela was my mum's name. I wondered if this was just some strange coincidence or else, some plan of Kyle's. Did he really think I'd open up to her just because she shared the same name as my mum?

"Hannah," she pressed. "I can tell your mind is racing. I've sat across from many people in that chair and I can tell when someone's mind is racing."

I looked at her. And then I looked away. Ten minutes to go. I wish she had just sat in silence and let me enjoy the last ten minutes of peace.

"Hannah…. What does he do to you?" she whispered.

My eyes flicked immediately towards her. *How does she know?*

"Hannah…. You know that everything you tell me is in complete confidence… right?"

She was giving me those sad eyes, the ones that looked as though she genuinely cared, the ones that looked as though she genuinely wanted to help me. God, she was good.

Finally I spoke. "Well, I guess time's up!" I shrugged.

"I'm in no hurry," she said softly. There was a pause before she spoke again. "I'm really worried about you Hannah. I can tell there's something really wrong. And I really want to help you."

I tried to blink back the tears which were threatening to fall. I jumped up and said, "Well, I really must go. I have to get home and get his dinner on."

She jumped up next to me. "Would it really be the end of the world if his dinner wasn't ready Hannah? Couldn't he make it himself?"

I humfed in response and knew that my body language was telling a million stories. The roll of my eyes, the anger on my face, the tenseness of my shoulders.

"What are you afraid of?" Angela asks. "By talking to me, what are you afraid is going to happen?"

And then I blurt it out. She's pushed me too far. I found myself saying, "He's probably got this whole god-damn room rigged and he's watching every word I say."

I could see the widening of Angela's eyes. Either I'd caught her out with her little plot with Kyle or she was surprised at my paranoia.

I could almost see the feedback she'd give to her supervisor. "Oh, I don't know how I'm going to crack this one. She's a paranoid mess."

"I've got to go," I said quickly and rushed out the door before she could ask me any further questions.

It wasn't until I was near the car park that I began to realise something. I fished around in my handbag searching for my car keys. Bloody handbag, everything but the kitchen sink was in here, I couldn't find the keys anywhere. I swirled my hand continuously around my bag and…. Nothing. I couldn't feel the jagged edge of any key. I began to panic. I stopped, set my handbag on the ground and rooted around it again. I moved objects out of the way and fished around for the bloody keys. Nothing!

My mind racing, I tried to think backwards. Well I drove

here, so I had them then. I parked up, I walked to the counsellor. Oh my god, I thought, dread enveloping me. Were the keys still hanging in the car lock? Had the keys really been sitting there this past hour or more, tantalisingly offering any opportunist to jump in and drive off in the car?

I felt a cold sweat drench over me as I hurried back towards the car in the car park, realising for a horrific moment that the car may no longer be there. How on earth was I going to explain this one to Kyle? He would absolutely murder me. There was no doubt about that. If drinking vodka on the sly warranted a wrist-grabbing episode, his car being stolen would surely tip him over the edge.

I ran, my insides panicking as I just needed to get back there and find out what was happening. As I was running, my hair bedraggled, my face close to tears, I could hear someone calling my name.

"Hannah! Hannah!"

But I didn't look back. I didn't care who it was. I was in no mood for polite small talk.

"Hannah!" The voice persisted, now running after me.

I ignored it and kept running.

And then I saw it. The car. Sitting there. Dutifully. Like a little lost child. Patiently awaiting its mother. The keys were still hanging in the door. I gasped with relief. Oh my god! For well over one hour, in a busy car park in Belfast, no-one has noticed the free car. I take the keys and lean against the car, overwhelmed with exhaustion and relief.

It's here. I repeated to myself. *It's here.*

"Hannah?" That same voice had now caught up with me. I looked over to see Guy standing there, watching me; a mixture of concern and amusement had crossed his face.

"Guy," I said, my voice choked with emotion. It was the timing of it; seeing a friendly face, after such a moment of worry, I was filled with emotion and couldn't help but let the floodgates break free. Tears spilled down my face and the next thing, he was beside me, putting his arms around me, hugging me.

"What's wrong?" he soothed. "There, there," he stroked

my hair. "What's going on, Hannah?"

So I told him. Everything spilled out. Maybe it was the relief at finding the keys; maybe it was my tiredness and exhaustion; maybe it was an hour of avoiding counsellor talk or maybe it was just his timing, but everything spilled out.

We got into the car, me in the driver's seat, him in the passenger's seat, and I began to tell him everything, about how difficult Kyle was to live with, about him threatening to strangle me, about finding my vodka stash, about his hand grabbing my wrist, about the counsellor, about feeling like Kyle was spying on me.

I took a tissue from my bag and blew my nose in a rather loud and unattractive manner.

Guy let out a long exclamation. "Jeez, Hannah, that's horrendous. I mean, I knew there was something wrong ... but this is…. this is awful!"

I nodded and looked around the car. "You know," I whispered, "I wouldn't be surprised if he had this god-damn car rigged either."

Guy looked at me and pointed outwards, indicating for me to get out of the car.

I got out and slammed the door behind me. Guy walked around to my side.

"Do you really think that?" he asked. "About the car being rigged?"

I shrugged. "I wouldn't put it past him.

Guy linked his arm in mine. "C'mon on," he said, an air of authority lacing his voice.

"Where are we going?" I asked, making sure this time that the car was definitely locked and I had the keys.

"We're going to the police."

I stopped mid-track and stared at him. "I am not going to the police, Guy." I announced sternly. I was surprised at my tone of voice. I sounded assertive, confident even. I never spoke to Kyle in this tone of voice.

"Why not?" Guy argued, his face full of disbelief. "The guy is an abuser! God knows what he'll do next!"

"Guy…" I said, in a weary tone, as though I was talking to

a five-year-old child. "What good would it do to go to the police? I have no evidence. Kyle could pay for the best lawyer in Belfast. He'll paint me as an alcoholic mother, drinking the bit out whilst pregnant with our baby. I wouldn't have a leg to stand on. And then where would I go? Not to mention what he'd do to me when he found me."

"But if you go home to him, I'm scared of what he'll do to you next."

I felt my inner resolve returning. I should never have told Guy all this. All I'd done was open a can of worms. My tone became cold and distant and I started to walk away.

"Guy, please, let me sort this out myself. I'm sorry I said anything. Please forget everything I've told you."

And I was off, walking back to the car, getting in it and driving away. I could still see Guy standing here, his expression puzzled.

But he just didn't get it. I had a child in my tummy who needed a father. I just couldn't do this.

***

"You took your time," Kyle said gruffly when I returned.

"Yeah, sorry," I replied quietly, as I took off my coat and headed towards the kitchen. I wasn't even going to explain myself. I didn't have the energy.

I switched on the oven and took some food from the fridge.

Kyle followed me into the kitchen. "Well, how did it go?" he asked.

Darkness was starting to fall. I switched on the kitchen lights and headed over to close the blinds. I saw a young woman walk past the house. She was looking in, watching us. I understood her nosiness. I loved this time of day, when it was too light to close the blinds, but you still needed to put on a lamp. If you took a walk, it was too easy to cast a furtive glance into people's homes, to catch a snapshot of their lives, to admire their décor and make stories about their lifestyles.

I bet she was thinking that we looked like the perfect

couple, the handsome husband, the housewife busying about the kitchen, the beautiful big spacious home with décor that looks like it's straight out of the Next catalogue.

Perhaps she was single, wishing she could meet a nice man like Kyle, someone who'd provide her with security ever after.

I snapped the blinds shut.

"It was fine." I had become monosyllabic. Any spark I once had was now gone. In its place was cold politeness.

"What's with the vibe?" he asked. He padded over to the fridge and pulled a beer from the shelf. *Oh, how I'd love one of those.*

My shoulders flinched as the sound of the lid cracking open went through me.

"Sorry, I think it just drained me a bit."

He leaned against the doorway, gulping back the beer. I was sure he was drinking just to piss me off, just to show me what he can get away with, when I couldn't.

He shook his head slowly at me. "After everything I've done for you. The counselling sessions I've arranged for you, this beautiful home I've bought for you… and look at you. A stinking vibe and an ungrateful attitude."

My insides sank with exhaustion. I really didn't have the energy for this right now. All I wanted was a hot bath and an early night. But I had to spread on a bright smile and act up to his paranoia.

"I am really grateful Kyle, you know I am." I kept my smile as genuine looking as I could.

"Show me," he said, his face full of mischief and indignation.

I looked at him, puzzled.

"Show me," he repeated. And then he took my hand, led me to the living-room, sat on the sofa and spread his legs wide apart. He unbuttoned his trousers and gestured for me to sit on the floor, in between his legs.

I wanted to gag, I really did. My head was whirring with indignation and anger. What husband would greet his wife home, after a gruelling counselling session which had drained her, knew she was tired and weary, and expected his wife to suck him off?

Kyle, that's who.

Again I could feel myself leaving my body. I watched the woman getting on the floor. I saw her sitting between his legs. I watched her perform oral sex.

And I knew that the whole time she was doing it, the only thing that helped her along was imagining that it was Guy she was doing it to.

Chapter Seventeen

Kerry

"Right, let's catch the bastard," Simon says as he picks up his car keys, and we leave the coffee dock.

"Barry and Peter, you tail me all the way and I'll wait for you just as we pull in."

"Yes boss," Barry replies as they power behind us down the corridor.

I can feel the adrenalin in the air, the excitement. The four of us storm out of the station and into our cars like men on a mission.

"It's always someone they know," Simon says, as he's driving along. "Someone close to them with a motive."

I know that he's psyching himself up for this. He's desperate to reach a conclusion. He wants to be able to close the case, to tick this off as another job done.

It's not just the satisfaction of finding Hannah and keeping her safe. It's not just the notoriety of being able to solve a difficult case. He's told me before about the pressures to get on top of everything. About how under-staffed we are and how many cases we have to deal with. "It's like a maths game," he'd said one time. "Reports you need to send back. Figures. Percentages of cases solved, percentages unsolved."

But now his hands are clenching the wheel; his jaw is distractedly chewing gum; he has all the pent-up energy of a policeman about to catch his killer.

We pull up near Kyle's house, parking along the kerb a few houses down. Kyle wants to wait for Barry and Peter. He says he wants to land in with the element of surprise. He doesn't want to give Kyle any extra time to get up to any tricks.

We see Barry and Peter pull up behind us. Getting out of the car, we nod quickly and we're off, charging ahead and making a beeline to the front door.

I rap the brass knocker. We wait apprehensively. Will he answer? Or will he pretend he's not in? I shiver slightly. I don't know if it's nerves or the sudden change in temperature. Winter is definitely on the way.

And then I notice a flicker of the curtains. I nudge Simon and eye his attention over to the bay window. I see a female ducking behind the curtains. Surely not Hannah?

Shortly after, I hear the sound of bolts being unlocked and then the door opens slowly. Kyle is standing there, wearing a strange expression. It's a mixture of surprise, annoyance and guilt.

"Hello," he says cautiously. He's wearing a t-shirt, pyjama bottoms and slide-on slippers.

"Mister Greer," Simon says. "May we come in? We have some further information to discuss regarding Hannah."

Kyle's eyes blink as though trying to adjust to the morning sun. "Er sure," he says, distractedly. "What time is it?"

I interject with the softest tone I can muster. "I'm sorry it's so early, Mister Greer. We … er… have a lot of jobs on today and this was our priority first call."

"Have they found her?" A voice emerges from the background excitedly. I can see further down the hallway there is a woman standing watching us. She is also wearing a t-shirt and pyjama bottoms.

My eyebrows raise. *Aye, aye, what's going on here then?* I think. *When the cat's away, the mouse will play.*

"Come in, come in," Kyle ushers, opening the door fully.

The aroma of brewed coffee and freshly cooked bacon greets us the moment we stand in the hallway. Seems like we've walked in on some cosy morning-after slumber party.

"Please, come in," Kyle leads us into the lounge.

We go in and sit on the sofa as instructed. Everything looks as immaculate as the last time, save for two cups on the coffee table.

"Would you like a coffee or anything?" Pyjama Lady asks.

"Oh yes, that'd be lovely," I say, getting in there quickly before Simon can refuse.

After taking our orders, she trots off to the kitchen while Kyle sits on the armchair and gives us an awkward smile.

"That's Julia," he says, nodding his head in the direction of his now disappearing friend.

"Julia?" Simon repeats. His question speaks volumes. He doesn't have to spell out the words, 'oh, so you're playing away the moment your wife's back is turned, then?' But it's obvious that's what his tone infers.

"Yeah, she's just a friend," Kyle babbles quickly. "She's been helping out with the Find Hannah campaign and things."

And things....

Simon nods as though pretending to understand, even though I know he'll be secretly storing the information in his brain marked as "another motive for Hannah's disappearance – so that Kyle is free to roam around."

"Mr Greer...." Simon begins.

"Please," Kyle interrupts. "I told you to call me Kyle." He smiles amiably. "Anyway, what is all this about so early in the morning? Have you finally found some info on where she could be?"

I find myself smirking. Kyle actually has the cheek to look hopeful and sincere.

"Ah, no... Kyle, that's not exactly why we're here this morning." Simon holds his black leather-bound case in front of him as though using it as a defensive shield. "You see the thing is," he begins as he slowly unzips the black case. The sound of the zip dragging along the teeth makes a screeching, unpleasant sound which cuts through the quietness of the room. "We actually need to do a search on this house this morning and we have a warrant to do so..."

Simon gives Kyle a serious look and pauses for a moment to let the message digest into Kyle's mind.

"Search this house? Why?" Kyle responds, indignant.

"It's nothing to be concerned about," Simon says. "It's a

routine observation. We simply have to be sure that we're checking all areas."

"What? But that's ridiculous!" Kyle says. "You mean to tell me that you think I have my own wife hidden in this house?"

The tension in the room is unbearable as Kyle's veins are practically popping out of his neck whilst Simon's face remains calm and serious.

"Here's the coffee!" Julia trills brightly as she saunters back into the lounge, ignorantly unaware of the conversation that has just ensued. Both Kyle and Simon adjust their body language as she sets the tray on the table and busies herself by pouring milk and asking, 'how many sugars?' and so on.

"Thank you, Julia," I say, as she hands me a coffee. I make special effort to mention her name, saying as Kyle hasn't even bothered to introduce us properly to his fuckbuddy.

She smiles gratefully at me and I feel a stab in my heart. I remember feeling like that. I remember one-night stands and that awful feeling the next morning when you knew you were a disposable object, someone that he probably had no long-term interest in.

"So, any news on where she is?" Julia asks brightly, sitting down on the other armchair and cradling a mug in her hands. Her face looks hopeful, expectant.

Kyle scoffs. "Huh! No!" he replies indignantly. "Detective Simon here thinks that I have my own wife hiding in the house and they're here to do a search on the place!"

A small gasp erupts from Julia's mouth. "Really?"

"Yes, really." I answer in a soft tone. "But we have tried to assure Kyle that this is a completely routine operation. We can't be seen to be making a full investigation if we don't search all areas."

I can see the logic of this settling in Julia's mind. "Ah right," she says. "I see."

Kyle puffs out an angry gasp of air. "I see nothing! Why on earth would I have my own wife hiding in my own house? That's so ridiculous! Why would I make the call? Why would I organise a Find Hannah campaign? Why would I do any of that?"

"Kyle," I say softly. "This is really just a tick-box exercise. We don't suspect you of anything." That was a little lie, but some lies are okay.

"And anyway, you have nothing to worry about," Simon says gently, "So why don't we just get it over with?"

"Because you'll wreck the place!" Kyle says angrily. "No! I won't have it! How can I contest this? I don't want you lot trashing my house!"

Simon then stands up and pulls the warrant out of the folder. Obviously he has decided the softly, softly approach isn't going to work. "Kyle, we have a warrant and we want to do the search now. So that's that. I'm going to call two other officers in now to help us."

And with that, Simon radios Barry and Peter and they're at the front door in zero time.

"Okay guys," Simon nods to us. "Check rooms as instructed."

And we're off. Simon had prepped us in advance on which rooms to check. It is up to me and Simon to check the basement. I've a feeling Kyle will follow us down and create a scene but if so, we have Barry and Peter on the other end of the radio. And anyway, if he kicks up a fuss, we'll know immediately that he's guilty.

Even when I'm treading the carpet down the stairs towards the door at the bottom, I can feel my heart fluttering. Will she be on the other side? Will Kyle come and try to fight with us? Even the thought of the enclosed space down below is making me feel constricted. God knows how Hannah must be feeling.

Reaching the door, I put my hand on the lever and surprise, surprise, it's locked.

"Kyle!" Simon shouts. "Key please!"

I knock on the door and call, "Hannah? Hannah darling, it's the police. We're here to help you."

I hear nothing in return.

"Kyle, the key?" Simon asks again, impatiently.

Kyle arrives at the top of the stairs. "Alright, alright mate.

Give me half a chance. I had to get the key from the kitchen drawer."

He steps down the stairs towards us and I can't help but feel panic rising in my chest. I don't like this confined space that we're in. I'm backed into a corner before Kyle. Kyle who has just been to the kitchen. What if he'd picked up a knife on his way?

He arrives at the bottom of the stairs, his face now level with ours. He's right up next to me, a smirk appearing across his lips. I can feel his breath on my face. A mixture of stale smoke, last night's alcohol and this morning's sex.

"Here you are," he says softly to me, his voice laced with sarcasm. He presses the key into my hand, his sweaty fingers lingering that little bit too long.

I resist the urge to gag but quickly take the proffered key as if it were a triumphant trophy.

Placing the key in the lock, I can feel my hands shake slightly with excitement and adrenaline. Maybe we hear nothing because he has her gagged. The key turns effortlessly and I can feel the weight of the handle as I push downwards. I open the door. It squeaks in response. As the door moves further ajar, my eyes try to adjust to the darkness.

"Is there any light down here?" I say, partly to Kyle, partly to myself, as my hand moves along the wall trying to find a switch. He says nothing, clearly unwilling to be in any way helpful.

Finally my hand settles on a switch and I flick it downwards. Immediately light fills the room.

I look around. My first thought is that there is no immediate sign of Hannah. There is no woman sitting on a chair tied and bound. All I can see so far are boxes, a bike, fold-up chairs, all the usual paraphernalia one would find in someone's basement.

I turn and look at Simon. He seems as disappointed as me. Then I catch a glimpse of Kyle. A sarcastic grin is plastered all over his face. He leans against the doorway and shakes his head, looking at us as though we're pitiful children.

"Oh dear," Kyle says sarcastically. "Looks like you're

accusing the wrong guy, isn't it?"

Simon ignores his sarcasm and replies. "We're not finished yet." Then proceeds to search in every nook and cranny, in every box, in every possible hidden space.

I radio to Barry and Peter. "Anything guys?"

They immediately respond. "Nothing as yet, we'll keep searching."

***

A full hour later we are leaving Kyle's house with no Hannah and a heavy heart. Kyle is standing in the door, smug as a cat who ate all the cream.

"You know Kyle," Simon says, a hint of annoyance in his voice. "We are doing the best we can to try to find your wife. And if you can't understand that means we need to search all areas, then I don't know what to say to you. We will continue to search for her."

"Thank you," Kyle says with absolutely no conviction in his voice. "I hope you find her quickly."

I can hear the door slamming behind us as we leave. I imagine how blue the air is inside now as he'll be swearing to Julia about what a bunch of timewasters we are.

When we get back inside the car, I can see the disappointment all over Simon.

"Fucking hell," he says.

"I know," I agree, softly.

"I really thought he had her."

"Me too."

Simon ran a hand through his hair. "Fuck's sake." He leans his face on his hand as though contemplating. "Where the fuck is she?"

I shake my head. "God only knows."

Then his hand lands on the steering wheel forcefully as though to let off some steam. "And how much of an arsehole was Kyle?"

"Well, we kind of expected that response, didn't we?

"Yeah, I suppose we did." He takes a deep breath, starts up

the car and begins to drive back to the station. "Fuck it. Fancy a pint after work today? I've just about had it up to here."

"Count me in!" I agree.

"Oh," he adds. "And don't worry, I'm not gonna make you pay for the pints." He winks in my direction and despite myself, I can't help but feel a flutter of excitement.

Chapter Eighteen

Julia

"Okay guys," the officer says. "Check rooms as instructed."

I look over at Kyle, my eyes widening. I can't believe this is happening. I can't believe that the police are here, in Kyle's house, about to raid it like some sordid drug den.

He looks back at me, his face like thunder.

I reach out a hand to place it on his arm, in what I hope is a comforting gesture. He shrugs me off and storms out of the living-room.

I follow him gingerly. I don't really know what to do with myself. Do I sit in the living-room and wait for him to return? Or do I follow him into the kitchen? Do we go ahead and have breakfast? Or do I just go home now?

I think longingly of the bacon and eggs that I've just prepared and my stomach growls. Wouldn't it be better if we just sit and eat our breakfast and then I can be here for him when the police leave?

I pad along the hallway towards the kitchen, feeling like I'm walking on eggshells. I can hear the police talking amongst each other. Kyle rattles around the kitchen drawers, cursing under his breath. I don't know whether he's talking to me or talking to himself. "The key. They want the fucking key for the basement. They think I have my own wife hidden down in the fucking basement." He spits each word out with distaste.

I decide that now is not the time to reason with him. Now is not the time to tell him that they're only doing their job. That they have to be seen to be ticking all the boxes. I remain silent and stand awkwardly by the table.

He storms past me again, still muttering under his breath. I can hear the sound of his heavy footsteps clomping down the stairs. I hear voices that sound aggressive and confrontational. Then all goes quiet for a while. I guess they must have got in through the door and now they're in the basement. I wonder whether she is down there. I'm immediately shocked at myself for thinking such a thought. As if Kyle would have hidden Hannah in his basement!

But if the police think it…. a little voice in my head says. *Then maybe*….

Minutes later, Kyle arrives back upstairs. He is still fuming, given the aggressive nature of his stance, but added to that, has a smug smile spread across his lips.

"Well…?" I ask, timidly, wondering what the outcome is.

His face darkens as he looks at me. "Well, what?"

"Well, what did they say?" I ask.

"Well, what could they say!" he responds. "Of course she's not down there! My god!"

He storms over to the coffee machine and picks a cup from the cupboard. With every gesture he makes, an aggressive force is added – the way he swings open the drawer, the way he rifles through the spoons to pick one, the way he slams the drawer shut again.

I close my eyes momentarily and remind myself that he is just stressed. That this is a horrible and stressful situation.

"Let's just have some breakfast and chill for a bit," I suggest, trying to diffuse the situation.

"I'm not hungry," he barks back.

Well I am…. I think, my stomach growling at me.

He runs a hand through his hair. "Look, Julia, sorry, but if you don't mind, could I be by myself? I really want some time alone after all this…"

I nod slowly, realising that this is his polite way of telling me to go home.

"Sure," I say, trying not to show how hurt I am. I also realise that I need to phone a taxi as I'm guessing he's not going to offer to give me a lift home. I can't even bear the thought of hanging on here any longer to wait for a cab. I just want out of here. The air is thick with tension and I long for fresh air.

Without another word I rush upstairs, get changed quickly, grab my bag and coat, and leave.

I don't even bother to say goodbye.

***

A few days pass and there's no word from Kyle. I continue to see news plastered everywhere about #FindHannah. Police say that enquiries are ongoing, and they are still appealing for any information possible.

My phone remains silent. No texts from Kyle. No phone-calls. No apology for the way he spoke to me.

Not until he's drunk, that is. Sure enough, on Friday night, at quarter past midnight, my phone lights up like the Blackpool Illuminations.

I open the text with a mixture of weary resignation and hopeful anticipation. Will he apologise? Has he had time to calm down? Does he regret the way he spoke to me? Or is he just drunk and looking for a shag?

Hey Julia x

I'm disgusted. No contact for days and then he thinks he can just type a two-word text and that I'm supposed to come running? What does he take me for? A mug?

Another text bleeps.

I'm really sorry about the other day. I was so stressed out about the police being there. I'm really sorry if I was grumpy x

I roll my eyes. "If" he was grumpy? There's no 'if's about it – he was a grumpy fecker!

A third text bleeps.

I'd really like to cook for you tomorrow night – to apologise. Please, Julia. Please forgive me x

I can feel my heart melting despite my anger. Jeez! How does he have this effect on me? How can he just click his fingers and have me come running?

But I can't remember the last time a guy cooked for me.

Actually, has it ever happened? I don't think so. I accept the offer just to see what he'll come up with. I want to make him go to the effort of juggling pots and pans, just as I had done for him.

I reply, keeping my response huffy and short.

Okay x

***

When I arrive at his house the following night it's a different Kyle answering the door. He is smiling, pleasant and relaxed.

"Come in! Come in!" he says excitedly, as he opens the door and ushers me into his large home. I walk in and he plants a kiss on my cheek, then takes my coat. I decide that because he's in such a good mood, I can afford a joke or two.

"I'll come in as long as I don't end up in the basement."

I look over at him, expecting to see him laugh in return, but I can see that the joke has fallen flat. His face is deadpan.

"Ha. Ha," he says, without any enthusiasm.

"Hmm, it smells lovely in here!" I say, quickly trying to change the subject.

I follow him into the kitchen, where an impressive spread is laid on the table. Fancy crockery, wine glasses and cutlery are neatly lined on the table.

"Have a seat!" Kyle pipes up, as he goes over to the oven and uses gloves to take out two plates.

Setting the plates in front of us, I marvel at the spread he has prepared. Steak, vegetables, chips. It looks and smells exquisite.

"Wow!" I exclaim. "You've excelled yourself! This looks delicious!"

I picture him spending all afternoon chopping and cutting and preparing, his shirtsleeves rolled up, his cheeks reddening with the heat of the oven.

He grins. "Well actually," he admits, "I got an outside caterer to do it for me. I'll be honest."

"You did?"

102

"Yeah! Me and Hannah did it all the time. It saves so much time and effort!"

For some reason I feel a glimmer of disappointment. I had expected him to want to spend the time and effort on me. Then again, he's gone to the effort of paying someone, what more do I want?

We lapse into small talk while we eat, and I begin to relax. This is fine. This is okay. Grumpy Kyle has disappeared. He was just stressed out that day. And why wouldn't he be? Anyone would be stressed out if the police landed at their door, threatening them.

In fact, the food and wine are relaxing me so much that I'm lulled into a false sense of security. I take his relaxed demeanour to mean that he's open to chat. I begin to ask questions about the police.

"What did they say in the end? When they were leaving? Did they apologise for wasting your time?"

He shrugs his shoulders non-committedly. "Not really. They just did their search and left. Arseholes."

"How long were they here searching the place?"

"Too long."

"Did they leave it a right mess?"

"Yep."

"Well," I say, scrambling for a question that might garner a longer response from him. "Did they say what they're going to do now?"

"Nope." He took a large sip of wine. "They're just a bunch of timewasters. They'll do a few tick-box exercises and then the case will be closed. They'll never find her."

I place my hand on his and say, "I'm sure they will Kyle."

He takes his hand away from me, picks up his empty plate and takes it over to the sink.

"Let's not talk about it anymore," he says. "Let's just watch a film and relax, huh?"

"Erm… yeah!" I agree, setting my fork and knife together on my plate to indicate that I'm finished. I'm actually not finished, but since Kyle has already upped and left the table, it seems a bit un-ladylike to keep horsing food into me whilst

103

sitting on my own.

He tops up our wine glasses and we go into the living room. I settle on one of the big recliner chairs, kick off my shoes and relax back. Ahh, this is better. Maybe we'll watch some nice romantic movie. Suddenly the night is improving.

Kyle goes over to his TV station and rifles through his DVD collection.

"Hmm, let's see…." he says. Then he starts reeling off names of movies. "I've got Goodfellas, The Shawshank Redemption, Fight Club." He lists some more but I'm quickly realising that there isn't one romantic film amongst them.

"I don't mind," I say weakly. "You choose."

He shrugs his shoulders. "Okay, cool. Let's watch Shawshank then. It's a great movie."

He settles down in the other armchair and the film begins. I can feel my eyes start to close with tiredness, but I will myself to stay awake. Instead I sip away at my wine.

Just as I'm noticing my glass is running empty, I notice his is too.

"Shall I get us a top-up?" I offer, getting up off my armchair to head to the kitchen.

"Aww, would you?" he says. The gratitude in his voice makes my heart melt. He looks so content sitting there, his feet up, his favourite film on, a glass in one hand. I'm glad for that one evening at least, the stress has melted away and his head is taking some time out.

"No worries," I smile.

"You might need to open a new bottle," he calls after me. "Corkscrew is in the drawer!"

"Okay!" I call back.

I go to the fridge and pull out another bottle of white. In a moment of nosiness my eyes scroll over the contents of his fridge. More bottles of wine, lots of meat, cheese, milk, bottles of water. He's certainly able to look after himself in Hannah's absence.

I go over to the drawer and rifle through the contents to look for the corkscrew. My hand settles on something. A small business card. I pick it up and look at the wording.

ARISE!

Women's Aid:

Helping women and children to stay safe.

I gasp and my fingers let go of the card as though they had touched burning embers. What if he came back in and saw me looking at this? What is it? Why is there a card about domestic violence in Kyle's drawer?

I shove it back in exactly the place I found it and retrieve the corkscrew. The noise from the TV is still blaring and Kyle is obviously unaware of my find.

My mind whirls as I open the bottle. What is it? Why is it there? Did Hannah stay there? Could Hannah be there now?

I pour the wine and retreat back to the living-room. Handing him his glass, I sit back on the armchair and we lapse back into watching the movie. The whole time, my thoughts continue to whirr.

What if she's there? Could she be there now? But surely the police would have checked all the women's aids? Or, if they're as crap as Kyle says they are, maybe they haven't.

My mind continues to spin. I wonder, could I go there? Could I ask them if they know where Hannah is, if Hannah is staying there or if she's ever stayed there? I wonder if they'd know anything.

Oh god. Where did it say they were? I only glanced at it, so I didn't have time to catch an address. I'll look it up online, I tell myself. I'll google it when I get home to find out the address.

My god. Had Kyle abused Hannah in the past? My insides writhe in disgust.

I glance at him. He's engrossed in the film, glass of wine in one hand, blissfully content.

His wife is missing, possibly lying in some rapist's den, and he's sitting here with me, drinking, blissfully content?

Chapter Nineteen

Hannah

"Hannah," the counsellor began, as she sat opposite me, the box of tissues on a table between us. "Last week you mentioned concerns about your privacy." She gave me that professional look – caring, sympathetic, warm.

I writhed in my seat. It felt too embarrassing to hear her repeat back my words to me. I said nothing.

"Hannah, that's a real concern you have. I don't want to dismiss it. I think we need to look at this issue before we try to go any further in these sessions – otherwise it'd be pointless."

I sat there letting her words sink in, not knowing what to say.

"Hannah, I am willing to move our session to a different location today if that helps you to feel like you're getting away from any recording equipment. I'm also willing to show you my outfit and let you see that there's no hidden recording equipment on me?"

My heart warmed to her a little. What a lovely gesture. She wanted to humour my paranoia by taking actual physical steps towards helping me.

"Okay then," I said, trying to call her bluff. I knew that she wanted me to say, 'oh no, it's okay, don't be silly, we'll talk here.' But actually I wanted to test her, to see how much she was actually willing to help me.

"Great!" she replied with a smile. She stood up. "Well," she began, moving her cardigan aside to show the material, "You can see that there's no recording equipment in here." She burled around to show me her back and lifted her cardigan so I could see the top of her trousers. "See? Nothing here either."

I nodded slowly. "Okay. So where will we go to talk?"

"Anywhere you want!" she said. "Anywhere you feel comfortable!"

"Alright," I said slowly. "There's a coffee shop on the corner. It's got nice comfy seats. I like it there."

"Let's do it!" she smiled. Then she added as an afterthought. "I'm glad you suggested it. I'm glad to get out of the office to be honest!" She had a little tinkly laugh which I found endearing. It made me warm to her; that and the fact that she was willing to humour my crazy thoughts.

In the coffee shop we nursed huge mugs of cappuccinos and began to talk. I told her about Kyle; about the jealousy, the possessiveness, about the aggression.

And then I told her about my drinking, how I hid bottles in the laundry basket, bottles in the hot press. How I sneaked a drink whenever I could, enjoying the feeling of the warm tingling sensation trickling down to my toes.

"I think I should take you to a twelve-step meeting," Angela the counsellor announced with confidence and I felt my insides wither. A twelve-step meeting?

"What, like AA??" I ask.

I imagined a room full of old men all sitting around in a semi-circle, all wearing trench coats, all hiding a bottle of whiskey in their inside pocket. I imagined long beards, a lack of hygiene, the down and outs of society.

I thought of my own home with Kyle. Our plush carpets which made your feet sink into them. Our large sofa in a 'L' shape where you could curl up and fall fast asleep in its immediate comfort. And I thought of Kyle with his workaholic attitude which meant that he had climbed the career ladder and created his own business with many employees out of hard work and long hours.

I was no scum of society. I was no alcoholic. Yes, I had hidden a bottle or two, but I wasn't lying on a street corner, about to sell my body for a cheap bottle of wine.

"I dunno…" I began reluctantly. "AA?" I mean, wasn't

that tantamount to thinking that the problem was mine, when in actual fact, I knew the problem was Kyle?

"Please," Angela urged gently. "Let's go to one meeting and see what you think of it. If you hate it, we don't go again, it's that easy."

I looked at her pleading face and, because I had warmed to her, because I had grown to like her, I found myself saying, "Okay then, one meeting. And you'll definitely come with me?"

"Definitely!" she smiled.

***

The AA room did have a semi-circle as I had expected. One small table was at the front with two chairs, and then a circle of chairs faced the table.

The AA room did not have a bunch of men in trench coats. There were men, yes, but there were women too. Women who were well-dressed and presentable. Women who were smiling and happy looking. These people did not look like the dregs of society. These people looked like normal, well-adjusted folks. Until they began to talk that is.

The woman at the top table began. "I'm Sarah," she said. "And I'm an alcoholic."

I was surprised. She looked about twenty-something. I had thought she was one of the counsellors, perhaps paid to lead the proceedings, but no, apparently she was an alcoholic too. She started to recount some of her memories, to tell us her story.

"I had run out of drink and I had run out of money, so I gathered all the empties that my flatmate had kept on the sideboard. I got all the little green bottles of leftover beer and I poured them into a pint glass. Then I topped it up with ice and knocked it back. My own lukewarm flat beer cocktail."

A ripple of laughter spread across the room. I couldn't believe it! They were laughing at her plight! But I had to concede that the laughter felt more like an identification laughter – as though they all had similar experiences and were acknowledging their unity.

I thought, with pride, that I had never compiled all the dregs of beer together to make a flat cocktail. I allowed myself to think that I wasn't as bad as this lot. You wouldn't catch me skanking around the bin. I drank the best wine and sometimes even champagne.

However, I did have to concede that sometimes my wine was lukewarm, due to the fact that I had to hide it in the laundry basket. But anyway, that was Kyle's fault, not mine. If Kyle wasn't so controlling, so possessive, so demanding, I would be able to drink as much as I wanted, at any time. I wouldn't have to go around the house looking for hiding places.

"I blamed my husband for my drinking," Sarah went on, her words alarming me. Was she reading my mind? How did she know that was exactly what I was thinking?

"I had an inkling that he was cheating on me. Silly things – hushed phone-calls, mysterious receipts; many late nights – his behaviour made me anxious and paranoid. So I had to drink. Well, that's what I told myself."

Yes! I wanted to say. *Yes, you're right! It was his fault! He did make you drink! Just as Kyle makes me drink. If he wasn't so possessive and jealous, I wouldn't have to drink. And then when I drink, it makes him angry – so the whole vicious cycle just goes around and around and around.*

"I had to talk to someone about it," Sarah said. "I had to talk about what was really bothering me – all the resentment, all the fear, all the things that were making me restless, irritable and discontent. And then I had to deal with it. I had to confront my reality. In the end, I had to leave him. That wasn't easy, but I'm dealing with it. I'm single, I'm managing my bills myself. I have peace and contentment. I can breathe. I don't need to drink today."

An appreciative round of applause spread throughout the room for Sarah.

Meanwhile I sat in amazed awe. Sarah had just told my story! My exact same story! And suddenly, I knew the answer. I had to leave Kyle too! But how? And when? How could I get away from him without him chasing me down?

Chapter Twenty

Kate

"So what are the plans for today?" I ask Guy as we sit at the breakfast bar. It's usually him that asks me this, but I'm fishing desperately for conversation. I can't bear the silence descending upon us. It's like an invisible heavy blanket; oppressive, stifling.

He shrugs. "Same old, same old," he says.

I sigh. It's like pulling teeth. Part of me is screaming inside. Part of me wants to yell at him, "Grow up! Stop huffing! Okay I don't want to get married but that doesn't mean you have to huff with me!"

But the other part, the kinder part, looks at him and wants to cry. He looks so pitiful, so emasculated. As though I've killed a little bit of his soul and now he's empty. I want to reach out to him, I want to touch him, to hold him. I almost want to say, "Okay then! We'll get married!" Just to put a smile on his face. Just to stop this horrible impasse.

But of course I can't, because that would be doing it for all the wrong reasons. And that wouldn't be fair on either of us.

Instead I reach for the marmalade and open the dinky little jar. I spread some liberally on my toast. When I crunch into the crispy toast, the noise is loud and jarring against an otherwise silent atmosphere.

Guy slowly turns the page of his newspaper.

Looking over his shoulder, I see another article on that Hannah girl. "Oh!" I pipe up. "What's the latest on Hannah?" I'm desperate for some conversation. Even if it means him just reading it out word for word, at least I'd get to check that his vocal chords are still working.

Guy quickly scans over the article and turns the page again. "Looks like they still haven't found her," he replies tersely.

I roll my eyes without him seeing. Finishing my toast and taking a last gulp of my coffee, I get off the bar stool and leave the kitchen. My heart feels heavy with this atmosphere but I'm too stubborn to confront Guy about it. Instead I brush my teeth, touch up my make-up, gather up my coat and bag, and make for the front door. I don't even bother to go back into the kitchen to give him a kiss goodbye. Instead I call out, "Okay, bye, I'm off, see you later!" I try to keep my tone as light as possible, but I don't even wait for his response. I'm out the door and closing the atmosphere behind me.

Getting into my car, I switch on the engine, and that is when I see him hovering beside the window, watching me leave.

I wonder if I should give him a little wave to show that I see him, but I decide against it and just drive off.

I throw myself into work as a means of distraction. It works. My in-tray is overflowing, and I have so much to get through that it's lunchtime before I know it. I dash out to a nearby café and grab a sandwich and coffee. I bump into my colleague Sarah and welcome the opportunity to sit down and share my lunch with her, grateful for at least someone in the world who wants to open up to me. She's telling me about her dad, how that he's sick in hospital with cancer. How's that she's been visiting the hospital most evenings to sit with him. My heart goes out to her. I remember the same scenario I had with my own dad. All those hours of sitting next to a hospital bed, the machines bleeping, the distress at seeing your own father looking so weak and vulnerable.

"How's things with you?" Sarah asks before she tucks into her sandwich.

"Oh, strange," I begin. I want to tell her all about Guy, about the marriage proposal, about the silent treatment, but something stops me. I'm wary of sharing any personal details with colleagues. I fear that gossip will circulate.

"Oh?" she raises her eyebrows, waiting for some juicy

gossip.

"Oh no, it's nothing," I shrug off. "It's just Guy, he's very quiet at the moment. I know something's wrong with him but I'm not sure what."

"Men!" she says, rolling her eyes. "They're all the same, aren't they? They keep everything to themselves." She takes a sip of her coffee and then continues. "I mean, my Kevin, I can't get anything out of him." And then she's off, talking about herself and her own relationship.

I'm both relieved and amused. How easy it is for people to lapse back into talking about themselves. How easy it is for me to body swerve my own personal issues.

Aware I'm zoning out a little, I can't help thinking about Guy. I know how anxious he feels about not bringing enough money in. I know how emasculated that makes him feel. But what could I do to help him feel differently about it, have his name signed on the house?

My insides felt queasy even considering that. An involuntary voice pipes up inside me. *Why should I? Why should I let him have joint signature of my house? What if anything went wrong? He'd get half the house.*

And there was the problem I guess. Wrecked with guilt, I realise that I wasn't willing to share half my finances with Guy. Does that make me selfish? Or scared? Probably both.

And what would happen if this silent treatment continued? Would we split up? Guy might just decide one day that he's had enough. That he might just get up and leave.

And that, I thought, is something I'd have to deal with if the time came. The thought surprises me. The thought of Guy ending the relationship and me not begging him to come back.

I return to work with a sense of resignation and acceptance. *Whatever will be, will be.*

Not realising it, I work much longer than expected. Darkness has fallen and the light from the overhead streetlamps can be seen.

Wearily, I pack up my things. I look at my watch. 7pm. Crikey. No wonder I'm starving. I wonder what Guy had for dinner. Checking my phone, I see a text from him.

Gone to the pub with Mick, see you later x

I notice the obligatory 'kiss' at the end. So he wasn't that angry then. But he's gone out to the pub probably to avoid me.

Sighing, I decide to pick up a takeaway on the way home. I can't be bothered to cook. And, knowing that I'll have the place to myself, I look forward to curling up on the sofa with a glass of red.

In the car on the way home I dial my best friend, Mags, on loudspeaker. She would cheer me up. She was my go-to pick-me-up.

I relay everything to her – the proposal, the silent treatment, the atmosphere.

"Oh chickie," she sympathises. "How awful. Poor you. And poor Guy. He's obviously just got his nose out of joint."

"I know," I agree. "It's just so bloody annoying though."

"Tell you what!" she chirps up. "Why don't you two come to stay with us on Saturday night? We'll all do something nice during the day – some nice fresh air, a walk. Then in the evening, we'll have dinner and drinks. Stay the night. We'll do a nice brunch the next morning."

I bit my lip. Actually that sounded like quite a good idea.

"Come on," she coaxes. "Between me and Mark, we'll talk Guy out of his bad mood. He can't sit around in silent treatment with you while we're there."

"You're right," I replied.

"Good, that's sorted then!" she cheered.

"Ah, hold on Mags, I have to see if he agrees to it first. He's so bloody grumpy, he'll probably turn me down."

"Hmm, well, good luck. Let me know what he says…" she tails off. "Oh! And if you do come, will you bring those foldable chairs of yours? And the sleeping bags? And that board game?"

"Anything else?" I joke. "The kitchen sink perhaps?"

"Ha!" she laughs back. "Actually we could be doing with a new one of those an' all!"

"Okay toots," I sign off affectionately. How she always

has the power to cheer me up, I don't know, but I love her for it.

Arriving home, it seems so empty with Guy out. *This is what it would be like if he left,* I find myself thinking. Then I scold myself for being so negative. For god's sake, he's not going to leave! He loves me! He just needs to get over this huffy period, I comfort myself.

I set my takeaway on the counter and decide I'll nip downstairs and retrieve the folding chairs and sleeping bags before I forget about them. I smile to myself. Obviously I'm optimistic that Guy will come away with me for the weekend if I'm already in preparation mode.

I arrive down the stairs and realise the basement door is locked. Bugger. When did I lock that? I run back upstairs and locate the key from the drawer in the kitchen. Returning downstairs again, I notice every creaking stair on the way down. I hate going down here. Not least because it's dark and creepy. But this is where mum used to live. It almost feels as though I'm prying; going back into her territory.

I slot the key in the lock and twist. The door creaks open.

"Hello?"

I jump. A woman's voice has timidly said hello to me! *What the actual fuck?*

I freeze.

Standing there, I feel fear wash up and down my body in a cold immovable grip.

"Hello?" she says again timidly.

I see her sitting there, on the sofa, her face almost as terrified as mine.

"I…What…." I can't get my words out. I want to say *who are you, what are you doing here?* But another part of me wants to run away as far as possible.

What the actual fuck is a woman doing in my basement? Locked in my basement?

"You must be Kate," the woman says. I can see that she's still sitting. She hasn't jumped up to come over and shake my hand. She is obviously as terrified as me.

"Yes… I … but who…" I stammer.

"I'm Hannah," she says, in a voice that sounds like a question. A voice that sounds like *Didn't Guy tell you?*

My feet manage to step over the threshold of the door, and I manage several footsteps until I'm leaning against a worktop, trying to prevent myself from fainting.

"Guy knows about this?" I ask, my thoughts whirring at a million miles an hour.

She nods. "Yes, he didn't tell you then?"

"YOU'RE Hannah?" I ask, incredulously. "YOU'RE the missing woman?"

Her eyes look somewhat amused by this. Obviously she is unaware of the news about her.

"Err... yeah, I guess I am," she says.

I look at her again. I look around this basement that my mum used to live in, my thoughts trying to piece everything together like a jigsaw puzzle.

"Guy LOCKED you in here?" I repeat.

Chapter Twenty-One

Julia

I'm sitting in a coffee shop, tucked in the corner, nursing a mug of hot coffee. Part of me regrets coming in here. I'm worried that someone will see me. How will I explain myself? Where will I say that I'm going?

I had opened my laptop at home and searched online. I did a search for 'Arise' and saw that it was on Fountain Street. Funny, the number of times I'd walked past it and never even realised it was a women's refuge. I had picked the little cartoon man up from the corner of the map and dropped him in front of the door – just so I could check the street view. I wanted to be sure in advance that I definitely had the right address. And there it was. Red door, number 19, with the smallest sign on the left of the door saying 'Arise'.

I felt I needed a coffee to build my nerves up. I wasn't quite sure what I would say when I got there. I couldn't exactly storm in and announce, "I'm here to find Hannah! Is she here?" Anyway, with such a huge missing person's campaign in tow, I'm pretty sure someone from the refuge would have told the police. Or would they?

Bollocks! I squirm down in my seat. I could have sworn I saw Kyle walking past! I feel my heartbeat thunder in my chest for a worrying minute until I'm sure he's gone past. I chide myself. I'm just being paranoid. Anyway, Kyle has loads of lookalikes around town – there are plenty of tall, dark men walking about.

I take a deep breath. It's now or never. Gulping back the rest of my coffee, I place a small tip on the table and leave.

I climb the hill towards the big red door, my heart

practically in my mouth.

Part of me wants to meet a heroic ending – find Hannah staying there, comfort her, inform the police of her whereabouts, be a shoulder to cry on.

But the other part of me fears a defensive woman coming to the door. Shooing me away. Spotting my nosiness a mile off.

Arriving at the door, I press my finger firmly on the doorbell, telling myself it's better to get it over and done with.

It seems to take forever for someone to come to the door. I stand in the doorway, my shoulders hunched up around my ears, hoping and praying that no-one will see me standing here. How on earth would I explain myself if anyone turned up?

Then I hear footsteps padding down the hallway. I hear a chain being unlocked. Then another chain. Then another chain. Blimey, it's like Fort-Knox here, I'll give them that.

The door opens slowly and only a fraction. Another chain prevents it from opening the whole way.

"Hello dear," a woman's voice says.

"Er… hello…" I venture.

"Can I help you?" she asks patiently. Her greying hair is neatly coiffed back.

"Am… I was wondering if I could come in. I need to ask you something," I begin hopefully.

The woman's eyes dart up and down the street. Then, presumably deciding that I look safe enough, she unlocks the chain and the door opens the full way.

"Come in, quickly," she ushers.

I dart inside.

She closes the door behind me, then begins her locking routine again. Lock one, lock two, lock three etc.

Finally she turns to me and thrusts out her hand. "I'm Mary," she says. "And you are?"

"I'm Julia," I reply. "Thank you for letting me in."

"That's okay," she says. "Why don't we go in here for a chat? It's a bit more private."

117

She ushers me towards a door on the left. Inside there are two chairs and a small table. It looks a bit like a counsellor's office.

"Take a seat," she offers.

She has a comforting granny look about her – pearls around her neck, a warm jumper, a tweed skirt, slippers. I could imagine her being a soothing mumsy figure for all the women here.

"Now, how can I help?" she asks, her face kind and gentle.

"Well," my fingers are subconsciously fidgeting on my lap. "I was actually looking for someone. A Hannah Greer."

I detect a look of recognition in her eyes, but she doesn't say anything. She remains silent and waits for me to explain further.

"You see…. I ah… I've kind of gotten to know her husband…. Kyle…"

Again I can see a flicker of recognition across her face. Her eyes seem to cloud over the moment I mention his name, but still she says nothing.

"… and ah. The other night I came across a card for this place in his kitchen drawer… and I suddenly thought… maybe Hannah is here…" I trail off.

Mary is looking at me with a glazed expression. As though she's still waiting for me to explain more.

"So… am… I'm sure you've heard on the news that the police are looking everywhere for Hannah and … I just thought…." My voice cracks with what I presume is nerves and embarrassment. I do sound nosy. I can hear myself. How long have I known Kyle? A matter of weeks? Yet here I am snooping into a women's aid?

Mary readjusts herself in her seat. She clears her throat. "Erm…. Julia…?" she asks, as though double-checking that that is in fact my name. "As you can imagine, we run a high priority confidential service here. We do not disclose the names of anyone staying with us."

I can tell that this is a well-used sentence. She has had to say this a lot of times. I wonder how many men have come here looking for their wives. I wonder how many men have sent female friends here on their behalf, looking for their wives. Maybe she thinks Kyle sent me here!

"Kyle doesn't know I'm here by the way!" I say, louder than I mean to. "I found the card in the drawer and, well, I put two and two together and...."

Mary nods slowly. "Julia...." She says, her voice laden with concern. "Are you in any danger at the moment?"

My eyes widen in realisation. Oh my god! She thinks I want to stay here!

"Who? Me? No!" I exclaim. "No, I'm fine! It's just..."

"Because if you were in any danger whatsoever, we would certainly try to help you." Mary offers.

I shake my head. "No really, I just...." But then I break off. Actually, why am I here? Is it really to find Hannah? Or is it to find out if Hannah ever stayed here? Perhaps what I really want to find out is if Kyle has ever abused Hannah, because if Kyle has abused Hannah, then surely it wouldn't be long before ... God forbid... he abused me.

"Actually... I kind of want to know about Kyle. If Hannah has ever been here, if Hannah has said anything about Kyle, if Kyle is the abusive type..." And there it is. My suspicions voiced aloud. My fears about Kyle. My theory as to Hannah's disappearance.

Mary twirls her pearl necklace absent-mindedly. "Julia," she begins. "You say you found our card in his drawer?"

I nod slowly.

"Has he done anything else to make you suspect that he could be abusive?"

"Well, no," I admit, feeling foolish.

"Raised his voice, acted aggressive?" Mary asked.

I shrug my shoulders. "Well sure, he comes across as a little aggressive at times. "

"Julia," Mary continues in her soft, sympathetic voice. "I can't disclose whether Hannah has ever stayed here, or whether Kyle has ever been abusive. But I will say this to you. If you suspect that Kyle has been abusive, if your gut feeling is telling you that something isn't right, then it probably isn't."

119

I'm sure she knows more than she's letting on. I'm sure this is her way of saying, 'yes, I do know about Kyle, and stay as far away from him as possible'.

"Okay," I say. "Well, thank you for your time." I stand to leave and wonder if I'll catch a glimpse of Hannah in the hallway. Perhaps I should ask to use their toilet.

But Mary steers me assertively towards the front door. "And remember," she adds as she's saying goodbye. "If you come into any harm, you know where we are."

"I'll be fine, thank you."

But the sad smile she gives me in return somehow makes me feel like I won't be fine.

I walk down the street, away from the red door. It is now dark outside. The streetlamps lighting the pavement. For some reason, I feel creeped out. I hug my coat tighter around me and walk as quickly away from that place as I can.

It's just that building, I tell myself. It's so full of negative vibes and sadness. It's rubbing off of me. I scold myself for trying to be some sort of Detective Debbie. Why don't I just keep out of it and let the Police do the work?

But as I walk along quickly and run for the bus which has just pulled up, my mind is racing. *What about the police? Shouldn't I tell them about the card I found? Wouldn't any information be helpful to them? What was that female police officer called? Kelly? Kerry? Perhaps I should phone her tomorrow morning and tell her about what I found?*

I will, I decide resolutely. *Tomorrow morning I'll phone Kelly and tell her. And after that, my police investigation ends right there. In fact, I think from now on, I'll take a huge step back from Kyle. There's something too suspect about him, I'm getting a bad vibe. And until Hannah is home, safe and sound, I think I should just steer clear.*

You see? I knew the counsellor's advice was a load of rubbish. I knew I should've just stayed safe under my comfort blanket.

I'm click-clacking up the road towards my house when I see a dark figure hanging around in my doorway. I feel my heart quickening, wondering if I've just landed home upon a potential burglar. But as I arrive closer towards the door, I can see the man's face highlighted by the glow from the streetlamp.

"Kyle!" I say, "What are you doing here?"

He gives me one of his charming smiles. "Aww, that's not a very nice welcome," he jokes. "I wanted to surprise you." He holds up a bottle of white in each hand. "Thought you might like a little nightcap before bedtime."

An awkwardness creeps all over my body. I don't want him to come in. "Oh, Kyle, that's really kind but, honestly, I'm exhausted. I wouldn't be much company."

I see the sides of his mouth downturn in disappointment. "What's wrong?" he says softly. "I've been texting you but you're not replying."

"I'm sorry," I squirm. "I've just been really busy Kyle."

Kyle's expression is full of sadness. "Did I do something to upset you?" he asks. "I'm really sorry if I did."

I have my house keys, ready to unlock my front door. Kyle is practically begging to come inside and giving me those sad puppy-dog eyes.

I reason with myself. Perhaps I've imagined some strange conspiracy theory for which I have no facts whatsoever. Even the woman at 'Arise' didn't admit to anything. What harm would one drink do before hitting the sack?

"Okay," I relent. "Come in." I put the key in the lock. "But it'll only be a quick one," I warn playfully as I push open the door. "I'm exhausted."

He's only through the door behind me when he pushes it closed behind. Half-jokingly, half-aggressively he replies, "a quick what?" He has pushed me up against the wall in what he thinks is a playful sexual manner, but it makes me feel claustrophobic.

His hands are on my breasts and his tongue is plunging, too forcefully, into my mouth.

"Kyle, stop… I…" I begin to protest but he ignores me.

"Oh Julia," he moans. "I've been wanting to do this all day." His groin is gyrating against mine and then he's carrying me into the living room, setting me all-too-harshly on the sofa.

"Kyle, wait…" I protest. But his hand has reached up my skirt and between my legs. He's pulling my tights roughly so that they rip apart, a sound that only seems to turn him on further. His mouth kisses hungrily more on mine. In hardly no time at all he's pushing himself inside me. Hard and fast and desperate. He's moaning.

"Oh, you dirty bitch," he's saying. "You slut, you whore." His words are hot breaths into my ear and I feel sick. Frozen. I can't move.

When it's over he sits on the carpet, panting. He looks at me, as though nothing is wrong.

"Fuck, you're amazing," he says.

"Kyle…." I say quietly, the shock evident in my voice. "You called me a slut… a whore…"

He looks over at me, his face full of remorse.

"Oh fuck, Julia. I'm so sorry. I couldn't help myself. It just came out in the heat of the moment. Oh my god, I'm so sorry." He pulls me to him and hugs me tightly, my head buried into his chest.

All I'm thinking is, *when can I get this lunatic out of my house? How can I get away from him?*

But something deep inside me knows that if I scream or shout, it'll alarm him. I need to play nice until he leaves.

And then first thing tomorrow morning, I'll be down at that police station.

Chapter Twenty-Two

Hannah

I went to more of those meetings. I sat and listened to all the stories of how others had hidden their drink. I listened to the woman who poured vodka into her pot noodle instead of boiling water, her kids wondering why she was munching away on pot noodles all day. And I listened to the woman who poured vodka into her iron instead of water, a hiding place that her husband would surely never notice. And I listened to the man who hid his drink in the shed in an old tub of turps.

I sat there listening to them speak and listening to how much they blamed themselves. They all thought that they were in the wrong. They berated themselves for drinking too much when it was obvious from their stories that they were just in pain. Often they had been abused in the past, or were in unhappy marriages, or simply found life too stressful to deal with.

One woman had stopped drinking but had then gone on to self-harm, finding another means to relieve her stress.

The more I listened, the more I felt angry. It wasn't my fault that I had been drinking so much, it was Kyle's. If he wasn't so jealous, so possessive, then I'd have no need to block out my pain. If he had remained the charming, charismatic man I'd fallen in love with, I'd be blissfully happy, content with drinking peppermint tea in the evening.

His aggression, his controlling behaviour, his need to dominate me, all mounted my frustration until I felt I had to drink.

So what now? I thought, as I sat and looked around.

The bunch of people in the semi-circle were all downcast, berating themselves, talking about how they had to make amends and live a spiritual way of life. Meanwhile, I was wondering how I could get revenge. What could I do to get Kyle back?

I found my mind floating off to a fantasy, one in which I hired a man to accidentally run Kyle over. It could be so straightforward. The guy would be driving along, take a wrong turn, and the next thing, smash! His car could ram straight into the back of Kyle's car. The Police and ambulance would turn up. They would pronounce Kyle dead on the scene and the Police would note that it was an unfortunate accident. The driver of the other vehicle (my hired man) would take a breathalyser test and it would be noted that he was stone cold sober. The event would be put down to a simple accident.

The Police would arrive at my door to tell me the bad news. I would act shocked and distraught but dignified in my response. I would thank them for coming to keep me informed. And then I would close the door and watch them drive off.

After they had gone I would do a victory dance and rejoice in the fact that Kyle was no more. The insurance company would inform me that the house and his bank account had been switched to my name.

I would attend the funeral and make sure that I saw his dead body lowered down into the ground. I would play the bereaved wife – dressed all in black, my face hiding behind a black veil. I would offer egg and onion sandwiches and thank people for their attendance, the whole time displaying a dignified grief.

And that would be that. Each morning I would wake up rejoicing that Kyle was no longer around. The house would be gloriously quiet. It may take some time to believe that he was never going to turn up, but after a while the tension would ease and a liberation would descend on me.

My fantasy was interrupted by a woman in the meeting saying, "Hannah, would you like to say anything?"

"Oh... hmmm... okay..."

She gave me a triumphant smile, as though she was pleased to see that I was ingratiating myself in her club.

"Well, my name's Hannah and I...." I couldn't quite get the word 'alcoholic' out of my mouth, so I said, "....and I drink too much..."

A murmur of approval rippled around the room as though the others were understanding of my denial.

"But the thing is...." I went on, "the reason I drink too much is because of my husband. It's his fault. He's very aggressive and...."

I noticed a woman to my right. She had that condescending look on her face. She looked at another member and they shared a 'glance' – a glance that said, 'Oh dear, this woman is in denial about her drinking. Obviously the problem is hers, not the husband's.'

So I clammed up the minute I saw that. I felt judged and looked down upon and I didn't want to open up any further.

"That's it." I said. "That's all I want to say."

"Thanks for sharing, Hannah. Keep coming back."

Keep coming back, I thought. *How fucking patronising. 'Keep coming back' means you're fucked up in the head. You better keep returning here as you're clearly a nut-job.*

I wanted to run away from the meeting then as far as my little legs could carry me, but I knew it would be too obvious if I bolted from the room, so I sat on, listening to the dreary stories. I started to count the number of times I heard 'I remember when...' and it saddened me. It saddened me that this bunch of people wanted to sit around talking about stories from years ago, over and over and over again.

At the end of the meeting a man came up to me. He said, "I was listening to your share. You know, it's not your husband's fault you drank. The problem is yours."

Well hello to you too, I thought. Where's the common courtesy in that? The first thing this guy says to me and it's an insult.

"Right," I mumbled and fled from him as soon as I could.

Outside, a bunch of people were smoking cigarettes. I

125

noticed a guy wearing a leather jacket. He had a long beard and was covered in tattoos. I had listened to him share and I liked the way he was as grumpy as I was. He wasn't one of these water-walkers talking about how spiritual and joyous and happy he was. He was grumpy, rebellious and indignant, like me. And not only that, but he talked about his past – the violence, the prison, the petty crime.

Perhaps he was my man. The one who could accidentally run Kyle over.

"I couldn't cadge a fag, could I?" I asked, sidling up to him. I hadn't smoked in years, but it seemed like the only way to strike up a conversation.

"Sure," he said, even though he seemed grumpy about it.

I took the proffered cigarette.

"It was interesting listening to you share," I said.

"Cheers," he said. "Just gotta be honest, you know?"

"The er… prison stuff…" I said. "That was interesting."

He laughed. "Interesting. That's a good word to describe it. It was nuts ."

"What kind of stuff did you do, if you don't mind me asking?"

I took another drag of my cigarette.

"Mostly drug-related stuff," he said. "I'm not proud of it but…"

"Have you ever…" I tried to build up the courage to ask him. "… done any favours for anyone?" "Favours?" he asked. An amused smile began to spread across his lips.

"Yeah, you know, someone paying you to do something for them."

I could see his interest peaked. He shifted his body language towards me. "What kind of thing?"

Chapter Twenty-Three

Kerry

"Another one?" Simon asks after he gulps the remaining liquid from his pint.

"Oh here, it's my turn," I say, reaching for my handbag.

Simon snorts. "Er, no. I don't want you slagging me off to anyone. Calling in the cash police!"

I smile at his in-joke. "Aww Simon, come on, that was different. I was talking about a date."

Simon stands up and looks down at the table. "Oh, isn't that what this is? A date?"

I can see the smirk on his face, his attempt at playful banter, and I can't help but notice my stomach flip at his mild flirtation.

"You wish," I banter back.

He rolls his eyes playfully and strides over to the bar to order more drinks.

I use the quiet time to pull out my phone and see if I have any messages. Nada. No-one wondering where I am. No-one wondering what time I'll be home. Nothing. Oh well. I watch Simon lean against the bar and notice the line of his backside as he leans forward, the ripple against his shirt sleeves as his arms bulge along the bar. I wipe away any self-pitying thoughts whilst relishing in this impromptu 'date'. Yes, I know he's a married man, I tell myself, but has he not just spent the last hour or so spilling his guts to me? Did he not confide in me about how stressed he was feeling, about how good it was to get everything off his chest? I savour a salutary feeling of accomplishment about how I've given him the space to off-load.

He returns with a pint of beer for himself and a glass of wine for me. Tucked under his arm are two packets of crisps.

"Look. Dinner too! What an amazing date this is," he jokes.

I grin. "The best!"

"We're going to be some craic tomorrow at work," I muse, looking at the empties spread across the table and feeling the effects of my head slightly spinning.

"Tomorrow is another day. Let's not think about that," Simon replies.

I look at him, a smile spreading across my face.

"What?" he asks self-consciously, noticing my smile.

"You," I say. "You surprise me sometimes."

He leans towards me and places his head on his hand. "Oh yeah? Why's that?"

His face is so close that I can smell him - a heady mixture of men's aftershave, his own natural smell and the faint odour from his pint.

"Well," I begin. "You're all Mister Official at work, but you know how to let your hair down."

His gaze lingers that bit too long, his face is angled that bit too close to me, his expression that has an air of seriousness, as though he might just lean across and kiss me.

"Oye, beakers!" A booming voice interrupts the moment and we look up to see Barry bounding towards us.

Bloody hell! Was he just about to kiss me? And what if Barry had caught us out?

"Barry!" Simon replies with forced joviality. "Come and join us mate!"

I smile broadly, trying to cover any traces of indiscretion. If Barry thought he was muscling in on us two about to kiss, the gossip would be spreading around Musgrave Station as fast as lightning.

Barry is chatty and jovial, and trots off to the bar to grab a pint.

I throw a sidelong glance at Simon, one that tries to evoke the impression of relief at not being caught out. But Simon isn't playing along. It seems that any earlier frisson of chemistry has completely evaporated. Either it was all in my mind, or he has chosen to pretend it didn't happen.

***

The next morning I'm sitting at my desk with a headache from hell. Why oh why did I have to drink so much last night? And on an empty stomach too. What stupidity. I am grumpy, tired and irritable. All I want to do is crawl back into bed and put this day behind me.

Just as I'm about to dash out to the shop to buy painkillers, my phone rings.

"Kerry," the receptionist says. "I've got a Julia Matthews on the line. She says she's phoning about the Hannah case."

My ears prick up. Julia? Wasn't that the one that was in Kyle's house the other day?

"Sure! Put her through!" I said immediately, trying to ignore my hammering headache.

"Hello, Julia?" I say, trying to keep my tone as soft and gentle as possible. I don't want to scare her off with an overly professional tone.

"Er, hi. Kelly?" she asks.

I give a gentle chuckle. "Yeah, it's Kerry actually, but you're close enough."

"Oh, sorry..." she says, sounding embarrassed.

"Don't worry," I say gently. "I've been called worse." I'm hoping that my light banter will put her at ease. I have a feeling she'll have something important to tell me. Why else would Kyle's fuckbuddy be calling me? It must be something useful to do with the case.

She laughs nervously. "Am... well... I know you're really busy... and I hope I'm not wasting your time.... but ..."

"Julia," I interrupt gently. "You're not wasting my time at all. Any information at all is useful to us, please."

"Okay," she says, taking a deep breath. "It's just that... well... in Kyle's house the other day I came across something...a card... like a business card thing... and well, it had the name of 'Arise' on it, which is a women's aid..."

"Oh right…?" I say.

"Well, the thing is, I visited them…to see if Hannah had ever been there… but of course they wouldn't tell me anything."

"My goodness," I say. "That was very brave of you Julia."

"Well, it just seemed strange to me, you know? Why would that card be in their house? And I wondered if Kyle would be in any way connected to … you know, Hannah disappearing…"

"Quite," I agree. "And ah… is there anything else that has made you suspect him, Julia? Anything else that he's done ?" I'm practically crossing my fingers, hoping she'll give me that titbit of information that might help us frame him.

There's a silence. Obviously she's finding whatever she wants to say difficult.

"Julia, would it be better if we spoke face to face? It might be easier than over the phone. You could come down to the station."

There's another silence, then a small, "Yeah, okay…."

"Okay. Well what time will suit you?" "Am… I could actually do about two o'clock today."

"Two is good for me," I reply, estimating that that will give me time to buy painkillers, neck them down and try to sort out this stinking hangover.

After making arrangements as to where and when we'll meet, I hang up and immediately phone Simon.

"Julia's been on the phone," I say, the minute he answers. I fill him in on the latest.

"Brilliant! Why don't you use suite C1? That way I can sit in suite C2 and listen in and she won't see a thing."

"Okay, great," I say, noticing a nervous fluttering in my stomach. This will be my first major interrogation where I'll be the only one asking the questions. And now the bloody boss will be listening in on me! Great! Pressure or what?

I grab my coat and bag and make for the shop. I need one huge packet of painkillers to sort me out.

***

130

"Julia," I say. "Thank you so much for coming in to see me." I usher her into the small room. There is only one tiny table and two chairs. On one wall is a dark glass window. Julia is unaware that Simon is sitting on the other side of that window, in another room. He can hear everything we say.

The last time I saw Julia she was slightly dishevelled looking. She was curled up on Kyle's sofa, wearing a bathrobe and no make-up. The Julia today has a completely different look about her. Full face of make-up, smartly dressed and hair neatly coiffed to perfection. But I can tell from her demeanour that she's nervous. The expression in her face is as one of a rabbit caught in the headlights.

"Please, have a seat," I smile, directing her to the chair in the corner.

"Can I get you a coffee? Something to eat?" I ask.

"A coffee would be great." She smiles nervously.

"No problem at all."

I poke my head outside the room and ask an assisting officer for some coffee and biscuits. Some small talk ensues for a while until we're settled with coffee in hand.

"Now Julia, I do have a couple of formalities I need to run through with you before we start chatting. This is nothing to worry about it and it's just standard procedure." I nod at her and wait for her to nod back to ensure she has understood me. "I do have to say that this conversation will be recorded – but it's only in case they need to refer to it at some other stage in the investigations." I then add in a jovial voice, "Most likely it will be filed away somewhere and never listened to again."

She picks up on my smile and returns it.

"Okay," I say, taking a breath. "Now, you were telling me on the phone about the card that you found in Kyle's house," I prompt.

Julia nods.

"Can you tell me a little more about that?" I ask.

"Well," Julia begins. "I just happened to be getting a corkscrew out of the drawer and I came across a business card for 'Arise'. I noticed that it was a women's aid and I

131

wondered why it would be in Kyle's drawer."

I nod in understanding.

"I thought maybe Hannah had stayed there at some point, otherwise why would they have that card?"

"Hmm, hmm," I agreed. "And then you decided to visit them?"

"Yes, I visited, and of course, because of their privacy laws, they couldn't tell me anything. They couldn't say whether Hannah had been there or not." She takes a sip of her coffee. "But I'm pretty sure if you guys went," she corrects herself. "I mean, if the Police went there, I'm sure they'd tell you more."

I nod. "We will certainly look into that Julia, and we're really grateful for you giving us that information." I pause. "I'm just wondering, was there anything else about Kyle's demeanour which made you think he could be the abusive type?"

There is a long pause.

"Well... yes..." she begins. "Last night.... He was very .... forceful with me.... verging on violent..." Each word seems to take forever to come out. She pauses after every few words. It's almost as if she feels guilty for talking about him.

"Forceful in what way?" I probe gently.

And then she tells me about how he pinned her against the wall, about how he forced himself inside of her. She told me the names that he called her.

Part of me is shocked, and yet another part isn't. How many times have I heard stories like this since working for the Police? And as for Kyle, I knew I had an intuition about him. I knew something didn't seem right. If he's capable of treating Julia like this, someone he hasn't known for very long, isn't he capable of doing the same to Hannah? And possibly worse. If he is responsible for Hannah's disappearance, then where the hell is she?

"Julia..." I say softly. " Has Kyle said anything at all which might lead us to Hannah?" All I need is for her to say, 'yes. Kyle confided in me'. But she shakes her head. "No, he's never said anything like that. He claims to have no idea where she is."

I can feel my heart sink.

"What do you think Julia? Do you believe he's responsible?"

"I'm really not sure."

***

"Bloody hell!" I cry when Julia has left and Simon has come into the room to join me. "So near and yet so far!"

Simon places a comforting hand on my shoulder. "Hey, hey, hey! Don't be so hard on yourself! You did great."

"Yes, but she didn't have anything. We're no nearer to finding Hannah."

"No," Simon agrees. "But we do have more info on his behaviour and it's all building a case against him."

"Fucker!" I say, remembering the way Julia recounted her experiences with him just the night before.

Simon leans on the edge of the table. "I'm pretty sure he's our guy – but it's how to prove it, that's the problem."

"And Julia doesn't even want to press charges!" I exclaim, throwing my hands in the air. "After what he did to her and she doesn't want any fuss!"

Simon remains calm. "You see it all the time I'm afraid. She's probably more afraid of what he'd do to her if he found out she pressed charges."

I shake my head, disgusted.

"I'm afraid you're gonna have to get used to this," Simon says. "Seeing pitiful cases like this and not being able to do anything."

"But we have to do something," I say, full of impassioned rage. "Let's go to that women's aid. Let's ask if Hannah has ever stayed there. It'd give us more evidence against Kyle. And then let's get him for a full interrogation."

Simon looks at me, his face full of something I can't determine – admiration? Amusement?

"What?" I smile, trying to detect his amusement.

He chuckles. "You. You remind me of myself at the start.

Full of passion." He gets up to leave, then turns back and adds "Don't ever lose that passion," he says. And then he's gone.

And that bloody flutter in my stomach has returned again.

Chapter Twenty-Four

<u>Hannah</u>

I tried to escape once, really I did. I don't want you thinking that I just stayed there, allowing him to treat me like that. Allowing him to make me give him blow-jobs just after I'd had a tiring counselling session.

I couldn't bear to look at myself in the mirror the next day. I couldn't bear the sight of myself. What had I become? What I had turned into? Was I really this much of a pathetic woman, who would allow myself to be treated like this?

I planned my departure carefully. I pretended like I was heading off to work like any other day. I put on my coat and placed my handbag over my shoulder. I gave him a smile and said, "See you later." He looked up from his breakfast and gave me a brief wave.

And that was that. I was gone. Out the front door, breathing in the fresh air, knowing that that would be the last time I saw him. I walked to the bus-stop and waited patiently for the bus, knowing that this would be the last time I made this journey.

And then I arrived at work. I had been preparing an overnight bag. I kept it hidden under my desk. And each day at lunchtime, I'd buy another thing to add to the bag – a pair of pyjamas, a toothbrush, toothpaste.

I worked my usual morning, knowing that this would be the last time I'd turn up for work. A feeling of relief and calmness washed over me. This was the end.

At lunchtime I walked out of the building and to my destination. People hurried past me, rushing to meet appointments, caught up in the whirlwind of timetables and stress and life. I just walked, peacefully, knowing that it was over.

I walked over the bridge and viewed the water below, the calm stillness, the overhanging trees. I wondered for a moment what it would be like to climb up onto the railing, to swing my feet over, to just let go.

I imagined the falling feeling, the feeling of letting go. I imagined how it would be if there was no more Kyle, no more walking on eggshells. No more pain.

But then I thought about my head crashing against the water and the sting of the coldness as my body submerged. And, of course, I thought about my baby. How selfish that would be to leave him. How selfish it would be to take him with me.

I kept on walking, and eventually reached my destination. 'Arise – Women's Aid.' They knew I was coming. I had phoned in advance. I had said to her on the phone, "I don't know if he's bad enough, if I warrant a place."

"A lot of women say that to us," she soothed. "But the chances are, if you feel unsafe and you feel you need to call us, then it's more than likely you warrant a place."

She led me inside, down a windy staircase, and into a basement.

"This is your room," she said. "You'll be sharing it with one other lady, but she won't be here for a day or two yet."

I looked around the small room. It had two single beds, one small wardrobe, a sink, and a tiny window. It was sparse. It was a world away from my bedroom with Kyle. It didn't have our plush carpets which your feet sank into. It didn't have our huge double bed. But I didn't care. A tiny single bed with no Kyle climbing in beside me felt like heaven.

The woman told me that dinner would be at 5pm. She said that there was a rota and that everyone mucked in and helped out. But I was exempt from the rota for the first couple of days. I was allowed time to settle in.

I sat on the bed after she left for what seemed like hours, thinking. My mind whirled with all the thoughts spinning around.

I thought about work, how they'd be wondering where I was. I thought about Kyle, what would happen when he'd return home.

I felt free.

I lay down on the bed and let my head rest on the pillow. I pulled the blanket over me and fell asleep.

***

It was only a couple of weeks later that he found me.

I stupidly had dashed out to the shop when I heard the quickening footsteps behind me. I felt the hand on my shoulder.

"Hannah, please," he'd said, quietly, sincerely.

I burled around to see his face.

"Kyle!" I blurted out. "How did you ...?"

"Hannah," he soothed. He wasn't angry at me, or threatening, or abusive. He was calm, gentle, quiet, as though he was a changed man.

"Hannah, I'm sorry," he said. "I'm so sorry." He took my hands in his.

"I'll scream," I said. "I'll scream, don't touch me." I pulled my hands away.

His face looked crushed with hurt and disappointment. "Oh my god," he said quietly. "You absolutely hate me, and I don't blame you."

We stood there on the pavement for what seemed like ages. He was apologising, and I was frozen to the spot.

"I'm so sorry Hannah. I've been thinking about everything, about the way I treated you. I'm so sorry. I'm sorry that you felt the need to run away. I'm sorry that you felt threatened."

His contrition continued. "I've thought about it all. God, it's all I've thought about. I'm going to change Hannah. For you. And the baby. I'm going to change. Please come home. Please."

I shook my head tightly. "No Kyle, I can't."

But something seemed different. He did look different. He

seemed calmer, gentler. Maybe it would be different this time. Maybe.

We talked for ages right there on the street. He apologised over and over again. Then he took me for coffee and we talked more. And then he took me for dinner and we talked even more.

Something had changed in him. He was softer, the aggressive edge gone. He was back to being Kyle – the man I dated, the man I first met.

I could feel my hopes raise. How I wanted that Kyle back. How I wanted the father of my baby to help. How I wanted to bring my baby up in a loving, secure, home.

"I'll come back," I said. "If things change."

His eyes looked hopeful. "Really Hannah, you will?" He reached over the table and took my hands in his.

"If things change," I repeated.

He looked at me, his face full of love and concern. "I promise," he swore. "I one hundred per cent promise."

***

Nice Kyle lasted for only a few weeks. It wasn't long before he was reverting to type. The old jealousies and insecurities returned. It seemed he was even jealous of our unborn baby, of the time and attention that I was paying to our child inside me. I spent hours poring over baby catalogues, looking at images of baby clothes and baby furniture. I read endless parenting books and tips on how to raise children. I was obsessed with learning everything I possibly could about how to look after this precious child.

I noticed Kyle's twitchiness quickly. I could see him watching me. One eye was on the TV, one eye was on me. I presumed he was jealous. I wasn't cuddling up to him, I wasn't asking how his day was, I wasn't rubbing his feet. I was focused on the baby.

It came out of the blue one day. I could hardly believe my ears when he asked it. He just blurted it out, out of nowhere.

"Is the baby really mine?" he asked.

I froze. I could feel my heart thumping inside my chest. I knew what this meant. It meant that the old Kyle had returned, the jealous, possessive Kyle.

"What do you mean?" I asked.

"Is the baby really mine?" he repeated.

I rolled my eyes. "Of course it's yours." I had allowed myself to become more blasé around him. Several weeks of good behaviour on his part meant that my guard had slipped just that little bit. "What on earth makes you ask that?"

"I saw you the other day," he said. "You were leaving work, with that man...."

I racked my brains. Leaving work with a man? I presume he meant a male colleague, and that we were having an innocent chat as we left the building. My brow furrowed, and I tried to remember who I had been talking to.

"Who, Guy?" I asked.

Kyle nodded. "Is that his name?"

I tutted. "Kyle, don't be silly. Guy is just a colleague, a work friend, that's it."

I was seriously beginning to worry about Kyle's mental health. He was clearly working far too hard. Lack of sleep and over-tiredness was making him a paranoid mess.

"Anyway, what were you doing watching me?" I asked.

"I had come to pick you up one day, I saw you both leaving the building."

"Kyle..." I said, trying to use as sympathetic a tone as I could muster. "Guy is just a work friend. You're being paranoid, honey."

"I want a DNA test," he announced.

I sucked in some air, surprised at his level of paranoia. Part of me wanted to laugh. Part of me wanted to say, 'Jeez, do you think if Guy was the father, I'd be living here? Don't you think I'd be living with Guy?' But of course I didn't say that. I knew that Kyle was on edge. I knew that it was only a matter of time. Kyle was reverting to his usual aggressive self. The act was slipping. Mister Nice Guy could only stick around for a number of weeks. Then the act began to wear off. He couldn't keep it up any longer. The paranoia and insecurity had crept back in.

I lay in bed that night, my mind spinning. I knew it was only a matter of time. Before long, Kyle would strike again. My safety was at risk. I had to make a plan.

But what could I do?

If I returned to the shelter he'd get to me. Could I find another shelter? Would they believe me? What could I say, 'he's being paranoid'? It's hardly enough to warrant a bed in the place, is it?

But I just knew. I could feel it in my waters. Kyle was changing.

***

I was right. Just two days later, Kyle's mood switched.

I was lying on the bed, one hand cupped around my swollen pregnant belly, the other hand holding a book. I was reading, content. My eyelids were drooping. I was about to let the book fall to the bed and lapse into a quiet slumber. Then I heard the sound of his footsteps stomping up the stairs.

"Hannah!" he called, his voice laden with aggression.

My tiredness immediately vanished and I was wide awake, on alert.

"Yes?" I asked, panic rising within my chest.

"Would you like to explain this?" He arrived through the door with pieces of paper in his hands.

"What?" I asked, completely confused and startled. I had no idea what he was talking about and the fear that had overcome me made it impossible for me to think straight.

"This!" he said, jabbing his fingers at the paper. It was a bundle of receipts and bank statements.

I looked at the papers, my mind racing, I had no idea.

"Let me remind you," he boomed. He held up one piece of paper. "Cashback!" he growled. "Twenty pounds." He picked up another. "Cashback. Thirty pounds." And another, "Cashback, fifty pounds!"

I could feel my heart hammering loudly.

"Would you like to explain yourself?" he shouted.

I sat there, mute, no words linking from my brain to my mouth. Fear prevented me from thinking straight.

It was the old Kyle, the Kyle who had found the Vodka bottles, the Kyle who grabbed my wrist and yanked it. The evil Kyle was back, like a switch that had flicked. He had returned.

"Kyle!" I found myself saying. "You said you weren't going to be like this! You promised!" I squealed.

He let out an amused yet angry guffaw. "I promised?" he mimicked. "Oh, so that makes it okay to steal from me then, does it?" On the word 'steal', he had grabbed my wrist and yanked me up from the bed, holding my arm behind my back.

"Kyle, no, please…" I pleaded.

His face was right up close to my ear and he growled. "Just what are you doing with the money, huh? Are you giving it to your fancy man?"

"No, it was just money for the house, for food and things."

He gripped my hand tighter and with each movement he was pushing me towards the landing. "Do I not give you money for the groceries?" he spat.

He pushed me on and I feared we were getting too close to the stairs.

"You do! You do! Kyle! Please stop this!"

But it was too late. In his angry, frantic state, he had pushed me. I lost my grip and I tripped, my foot not making it to the step. I crashed all the way down the stairs in one swift, flying movement.

***

When I came to there was blood everywhere, up the walls, along the carpet, a sea of red everywhere. Somehow I crawled along and grabbed the phone. I dialled 999. Everything happened so quickly.

"Ambulance please."

A calm woman's voice asked something. It was all too fast

for me to remember.

"There's blood everywhere. And I'm pregnant," I said, my voice much calmer than I felt.

I remember her soothing voice. I remember I could hear her sympathy. I remember her saying something about opening the curtains and putting on the light so that the ambulance men could see me. I remember her saying, "You're going to be okay."

I didn't believe her, but I appreciated her concern.

Kyle was squirming in the corner. The switch had flicked. He was back into remorseful mode. It's as if the push had gotten all that aggression out of his system. And then when he saw his bleeding wife, the aggression passed, and remorse kicked in.

I lay on the floor, my face along the carpet. I looked at all the blood. I rocked myself back and forth. "My baby," I cried. "My baby." And I just knew that in all that blood, my baby was gone.

Chapter Twenty-Five

Hannah

When I come to in the hospital, I see a large clock on the wall. I can hear a cheerful nurse. She's on the phone to someone. She sounds so happy, so full of life.

The walls look fuzzy. Then a face comes into my view. It must be a nurse.

"Mrs Greer," she's saying. "Glad to see you coming round."

My brain is too foggy to know what she's talking about. It's as if I've been in a very long tunnel and now I'm out in the light and I've no idea what happened.

I turn my face to the right. I see a bed next to me. I see a man lying on the bed. His head is wrapped with a lot of bandages. Ouch. That looks painful. A team of nurses and doctors surround him. They're saying things like, "The surgery was successful" and "We managed to get it all out of your brain."

I realise I'm in a recovery room. What happened? Oh yes, the accident. Falling down the stairs. Kyle. My baby.

"My baby!?" I cry. "What about my baby?"

The nurse tries to soothe me. "Mrs Greer, you're awake. You're okay. You're okay."

But I know I'm not okay. I'm far from okay.

"The baby has gone hasn't he? He's gone," I cry.

"You're okay," the nurse soothes again. "The doctor will come to speak to you shortly." She places a comforting hand on mine. "And your husband's on his way too."

She says this as though it's a good thing. I groan. I don't want to see Kyle. He is the last person I want to see.

"Hello, I'm Doctor Patterson," a kindly looking man says to me, when I'm back in a hospital ward. "You probably don't remember talking to me earlier – when you were coming out of the anaesthetic…"

He looks so young, this doctor, so fresh-faced, so innocent.

"Mrs Greer, I'm terribly sorry, but you did lose the baby."

There we have it. Blunt as you like. Straight and to the point.

"The fall down the stairs was too traumatic and the stress on your abdomen was too severe."

I can feel the tears starting to spring into my eyes.

"However," he rattles on. "There are thankfully no broken bones, only some minor fractures which we will keep an eye on. I'd like you to stay here in hospital for a few days while we keep an eye on you."

I lean my head back on my pillow and close my eyes. My baby, gone.

"Oh, look, you have a visitor," the doctor announces, and I hear the sound of footsteps draw closer to my bed.

I open my eyes to see a smiling face looking down on me. It is a face full of compassion, but a face that turns my stomach. Kyle.

"Hey, sweetie," he says in a cooing, gentle tone, which I'm sure is intended for the benefit of the doctor.

I don't reply.

"Well," the doctor says, "I'll leave you two in peace. I'll check on you later, Mrs Greer, okay?"

I nod, and he's gone. And then it's just me and Kyle. He is sitting on the chair next to me, smiling like an over-sympathetic goon.

"I brought you some things." He holds up a plastic bag full of something and begins to take stuff out of it – a magazine, some chocolates, a bottle of sparkling water and some grapes.

I don't say anything.

He has that awkward smile on his face. It is a smile that

says he knows he's in the wrong, he's full of remorse, and he's hoping I'll forgive him.

I don't smile back.

"How are you feeling sweetie?" he asks, with that pathetic, fake kindness which I know is forced.

"Terrible," I reply. "I've lost the baby."

He gives me a small sympathetic nod. Obviously the doctor had filled him in before he got here.

"I know. I'm so sorry," he whispers.

"And it's your fault," I whisper back, between gritted teeth.

This is the first time I've ever spoken back to him. I'm shocked at my bravery. But then again, it's easy to be brave when I'm lying on a hospital bed, when I know that I have a red alarm button in front of me. One little squeeze of my finger and a nurse would come running.

He hangs his head in shame like a pitiful puppy. "I'm so sorry," he whispers. "It was an accident. You slipped."

"I. Didn't. Slip." I say, between gritted teeth. "You. Pushed. Me."

I see his eyes cloud over. The old Kyle is returning, the defiant Kyle.

"You slipped," he repeated. "And it's your word against mine." His voice is low, his tone gentle, but his words are stinging.

My finger presses the button of its own accord. A nurse comes running.

"Is everything okay, Mrs Greer?" a young woman in a blue nurse's tabard asks.

"I just really want to be left alone now. Can I have no more visitors please?"

I close my eyes and can hear the nurse usher Kyle out of the ward. Oh, how I would have loved one of these red buttons when I lived with him.

I fall into a slumber and when I awake later, I see another face staring down at me. This time, I'm happy to see who it is.

"Guy…" My throat croaks with relief and a smile spreads

over my face. "Guy."

"Hello you," he soothes.

I reach out and take his hand. "How did you know where I was…?"

"Oh, you know," he jokes. "Just keeping up with my usual stalking procedures."

I give a small laugh, the first one in what seems like ages.

"Oh Guy…" I say. "I'm a mess…"

He squeezes my hand. "What did he do to you?" he asks, his face wincing.

I tell him everything that had happened since that day when Guy wanted me to go to the police, when Guy was worried that Kyle would abuse me further.

"And now I've lost the baby," I say, finishing my tale.

I see Guy's jaw clench. "That fucking bastard."

I'm too tired to argue.

"We have to tell the police," Guy says resolutely.

"Guy, no…" I begin. I don't have the energy for this. I don't have the energy for police statements or interrogations. And I certainly don't have the energy for the backlash from Kyle. Kyle would not go quietly. Kyle would probably say that I'd had too much to drink and that I slipped. He probably has hidden camera footage of me hiding the bloody drink.

"Hannah, no. He can't get away with this."

"I don't have the energy, Guy. "

He bites his lip, realising that he's getting too het-up. He can see my exhaustion.

"Sorry," he says. "You're just out of surgery and I'm ranting like an asshole."

I smile at him. "Just a tiny bit of an asshole. "

"Can I get you anything?" he asks, changing the subject.

"No, I'm okay."

"Come and live with me," Guy says suddenly, his face earnest.

"What?" I ask, surprised.

"Come and live with me," he repeats. "We have a basement downstairs. Kate's mum used to live in it. You can stay there. You'll be safe."

I shake my head slowly. "But what about Kate? She wouldn't like some other woman living in her house."

He shrugs his shoulders. "She'll get over it. I'll explain the situation to her."

I shake my head again. "No. He'd find me. And then he'd just torture you. Or torture me to return."

"So we won't tell him," Guy shrugs.

I'm too tired to think straight. My head is swimming. Could this actually work?

"Look," Guy says. "The offer's there. Bear it in mind." He rests his hand on mine. "Try and get some sleep, huh? I'll come back again tomorrow."

I want to grab on to his hand. I want to make him stay, for him to sit there beside me and to protect me. But of course I know that's silly.

"Okay." I smile. "See you tomorrow."

And then he's gone. I'm watching his back as he walks out of the ward.

**

An emptiness descends over me after he leaves. There's a quietness save for the beeping of the machines and the distant voice of nurses in other wards. There's just this nothingness. I lie there, staring out the window, seeing the high-rise buildings outside, looking at the four walls of the hospital ward.

A dull emptiness washes over me. The baby has gone and it's my fault.

I should've protected him. I should've left Kyle ages ago. I should never have returned to him that time after the women's aid. Why did I go back? Did I honestly think that he would change?

Depression descends over me like a lead blanket. It is a heavy weight under which I cannot move.

What was there left to live for?

The baby had gone. I hadn't protected it. I had no desire to live with Kyle, and yet I knew he wouldn't let me go without a fuss. Kyle wouldn't allow me to report him to the police. And if I did report him to the police, he would fight his corner and tell them that I was drunk and had slipped. It would be his word against mine, and Kyle could afford a better lawyer than me.

It felt like I had a huge mountain to climb, the mountain of reporting Kyle, leaving Kyle and starting my life afresh. I didn't have the energy for any of it.

I prayed that I could just close my eyes and never wake up, that I would never have to face another day.

I felt tears rise and then spill down my cheeks. Like a tap that had just been turned on, the tears gushed out. A nurse came to my side and then a doctor shortly after that. Tablets were prescribed and then a glass of water appeared. I knocked the tablets back not even caring what they were. The nurse said that they would help me calm down, so I took her word for it.

The calmness did come, like a bunch of cotton wool that was wrapped around me. I wanted that cotton wool feeling to last forever. I closed my eyes and slept.

Chapter Twenty-Six

Kate

"Guy locked you in here?" I repeat.

"Well, ahh…" she stammers.

My hand reaches immediately for my phone which is in my back pocket. With trembling fingers, I dial Guy.

"Yup," he answers casually.

"What. The. Actual. Fuck?" I spit out.

"Huh?"

"Get home right now. I swear to God. What the fuck is Hannah doing in our basement?"

"Kate, please calm down," Guy says. "I can explain."

"You can explain?" I retort. "You can explain? Well you better have a bloody good explanation for why you have a woman locked in our basement Guy! That's a new one on me!"

"It's not what you think," Guy says. "It's not how it looks."

I let out a laugh. "Jesus, I've heard about this! *It's not how it looks?*' That's the oldest trick in the book!"

All my insecurities, all the fears that I've ever had about relationships are rushing back at me full fold. The number of times you heard stories where a woman thought she was blissfully in love with a man and then finds him in bed with someone else, how he always says those clichéd statements like 'it's not how it looks'.

"I'll tell you how it looks, Guy!" I continue. "I've come home to find that you've locked another woman in our basement! How else can that look?"

"But you don't understand. She wants to be there!"

"Jesus, you are so full of shit! Get home now!"

"Oh… ah…" he says slowly. "Okay, I'll be home shortly."
He hangs up. I can picture him downing the last of his pint
for Dutch courage.

My mind is spinning, I can hardly think straight. This is
why I didn't accept his proposal of marriage. This is the very
thing I feared. This is the reason you shouldn't trust. You
never know what you will come home to.

I try to calm myself down. My body is pumping with
anger and, despite the fact that I want to kill Guy, I'm aware
that just across the room is some poor victim who has been
locked up for weeks.

"Hannah," I say, crossing the room tentatively to her. "Are
you okay? I can't believe he's had you locked down here."

She smiles timidly. She looks terrified of me.

I sit down on the sofa next to her. She looks so frail, so
weak.

"What has he done to you?" I ask quietly.

She raises a hand to her mouth, subconsciously placing the
tip of her thumb in her mouth, as though wondering what to
say.

Eventually she speaks.

"Please don't tell anyone about this," she croaks.

"I'm gonna fucking kill him, that's what I'm gonna do!" I
say, anger bursting out of my chest. How dare Guy do this to
her. What was he thinking? And what was all that bollocks
about him wanting to marry me when he had a woman
locked in our basement all along? It's ridiculous, Like
something out of a TV drama!

She shakes her head. "No, no, please don't do that!"

I look at her, incredulous. How could she be so calm?
How come she wasn't running for the door, dying to get
away from here, dying to phone the police and report Guy?

My head hurt with how much it was spinning.

Hannah finally speaks again. It's as if all this time being
trapped alone has turned her into a mute person, and now
she's trying to remember how to use her voice.

"I really don't want the police to know," she persists. "If

you tell them, it'll only make it more difficult for me, and for you too. He'll come after both of us, I swear."

Her words are like a blow to my chest. Would he come after both of us? How much of an animal has Guy been to her? Who is this ogre I've been living with, this monster that I've been sharing a bed with?

"Hannah," I beg. "Please tell me, what did he do to you?" I want to know, and yet I don't want to know. I don't want to know about how he's been raping her, or physically abusing her, or whatever the fuck he's been doing to her whilst she's been trapped in this basement. I don't want to know that the man I thought loved me was actually a secret rapist.

Hannah tells me. She tells me about losing the baby, about him pushing her down the stairs, about losing all the blood, about the women's refuge, about him begging her to return, about her going back to him, about the abuse happening all over again.

I listen, shocked and confused.

"Wait…" I say. "But what about Guy? Why has he locked you in here? What has he been doing to you?"

Hannah looks at me, startled. "Guy?" she says, her brow furrowing in confusion. "He's done nothing to me."

I sit there, confused, all the pieces of the jigsaw slowly fitting together. So she's talking about her husband Kyle abusing her. Meanwhile, I'm thinking that it's Guy abusing her.

The final piece of the jigsaw slots into place as I come to the conclusion. "So Guy was keeping you safe down here?"

She nods, slowly. "Yes. I've been hiding."

I take a huge breath, realising that it's one of relief. Thank god! So Guy isn't the serial killing rapist that I thought he was!

I look at Hannah, her fingers squeezing a tissue with such ferocity that it is now in a tiny clump in her hands. She's a nervous wreck. And now I've landed down here, asking her a million questions and possibly threatening her hiding place.

I shake my head slowly. "I can't believe you've been hiding down here all this time," I say.

She looks at me, her face a mixture of fear and guilt. "I'm sorry," she says. "I really am sorry. I had nowhere else to go."

My heart opens like a gentle flower. How could I be angry with her? This poor woman, hiding here in this basement, by choice, having lost her baby, and terrified that her husband would find her.

"Oh Hannah," I say. "Don't apologise." She's so tiny, so frail. "Can I give you a hug?"

"Er… yeah."

I lean over and hug her. She's as stiff as a board. Her body is full of tension and anxiety.

When I pull away, I want to check one last thing with her. "Hannah please promise me. Guy hasn't hurt you in any way, has he? He hasn't made any moves on you?"

She shakes her head resolutely. "No, I promise," she says. And I can tell she means it.

***

"Ah, you've met then," Guy says with forced joviality when he finally walks in the door.

Hannah and I are sitting side by side on the sofa, chatting, a cuppa each in our hands.

Even though Hannah has filled me in on the full story, even though I know that Guy isn't to blame, I'm still annoyed at his blasé behaviour. How dare he saunter in through the door as though he's done nothing wrong, as though he can just swoop in like some heroic finale and not have to explain himself?

"No thanks to you," I say, my voice laden with disgust. "You could have introduced me weeks ago, instead of hiding someone in the floor below us, without telling me anything."

His smile quickly drops, and he stands here, awkwardly.

I set my cup on the side table and stand up, crossing over to him.

"Guy," I seethe. "Why didn't you tell me? I can't believe you kept such a huge secret like that from me?"

I'm aware that Hannah is squirming in the corner, probably feeling guilty for having caused this marital tiff.

"I couldn't tell anyone," Guy says defensively. "If I told you then you might have felt you had to tell the police. And Hannah didn't want the police to know."

"But," I argue "How could you want to marry me when we had this huge secret from each other? It's preposterous!"

Guy shrugs his shoulders and thrusts his hands into his pockets. "I don't know. I was just trying to help Hannah, that's all."

I'm standing here, my gaze shifting between Guy, who is standing, looking uncomfortable, and Hannah, who is sitting on the sofa looking equally as awkward.

"And what are we going to do about the police?" I ask.

They both look sharply at me, and I can see the fear in their eyes.

"No, please…" Hannah begins. "Please don't tell them."

I go back to my sitting position on the sofa. "But Hannah, you can't keep this secret. Just think of how much police time is being spent on looking for you."

Guy rolls his eyes. "Oh don't pile the guilt on her, Kate. Don't you think she's been through enough? And anyway, what police time? They probably spent two minutes on the case and then moved on to something else."

"Guy!" I cry. "Are you mad? If the police find out that we've been hiding her all along, do you know how much trouble we'll be in? We can't do it!"

Hannah puts her head in her hands. Obviously her worst fears have been confirmed. I have found her. I'll tell the police.

"Hannah," I say, placing a hand on her back. "We have to tell them. But they'll protect you! Just tell them everything about Kyle. They'll protect you!"

She shakes her head. "No they won't. They'll just do a load of paperwork and Kyle will be set free. He'll find me wherever I end up living and that will be the end."

I take a huge breath and can see her fear. It's as visible as a lead blanket. But I'm full of fear too. If the police keep spending more time and money searching for Hannah, and yet we have her all along, what will happen to us?

"I'm sorry." I announce. "I have to tell them." I take my phone out of my back pocket and begin to dial 999.

"Kate, no," Guy says loudly.

"Yes," I argue.

My fingers are hitting the buttons quickly. "Police please," I say. I'm driven by fear. I want it to be recorded that the moment I found out about Hannah, I reported it. I'm not leaving it another day.

Guy is holding his head in his hands. "Sorry, Hannah," I hear him whisper.

Hannah is curling up into a foetal position on the sofa.

"Er yeah. I'm phoning about that missing person, Hannah Greer. I've just found her."

Chapter Twenty-Seven

Kerry

Simon and I climb the steep hill towards number 19.

"Jeez, could this street be any more difficult to climb?" I moan, realising that I really need to gym it a bit more, my fitness is flagging.

"Come on granny, keep up," Simon jokes in his usual banter.

I groan. "You can talk, grand-dad. What age are you again?"

He tuts and gives me a playful swipe on my arm.

As we approach the red door, we lapse into a more reverent silence. It seems wrong to be jolly and jesting when we're about to visit a women's aid.

Arriving at the door, both dressed in our uniformed attire, I notice the blinds twitch and a woman's face peeking out. I can't help but notice the large blackish-purplish bruise that surrounds her left eye.

My stomach lurches, anger rising in my belly. Who is the bastard that did that to her, I wonder.

The blinds quickly snap shut and she recoils away from the window. We have this effect on people. The minute they spot our uniform they hide away, as though they have something to feel guilty about.

Simon knocks on the door loudly and we wait. I can hear footsteps approaching and then a series of bolts and chains being unlocked.

A mumsy-looking older woman opens the door. She gives a tentative smile.

"Hello officers," she says. "How can I help you?"

"Hi there," I smile. "We were just wondering if we could

come in and speak to you for a few minutes. Are you the manager here?"

"Yes," she says slowly. "I'm Mary." Then she pauses, looking sceptical. "What's wrong?"

I hold up my identification badge. "We just have a few questions in connection with the disappearance of Hannah Greer. May we come in?"

Mary pauses, but then stands back to let us enter. "Come in," she says.

"Thank you."

We walk past her and into a hallway. I see a woman scarper from one door and hurry off down the corridor. She looks terrified. Pale, waif-like, with a huge cardigan wrapped around her.

Mary leads us into a small room. There are two chairs and a small table.

"Take a seat," she says. "I'll go and get another chair."

We sit down and wait until she returns.

Simon gives me a look and already I'm learning how to read his mind. He looks uncomfortable, as though the surroundings are making him feel both sad and angry. How any man could treat a woman so badly that she'd be subjected to having to hide away in a place like this, is probably the thought running through his head.

Mary returns with another chair and offers us a coffee.

"Oh no, it's fine. Don't go to any trouble," I tell her.

"It's no trouble," Mary says. "One of the girls will be happy to help."

I throw a sidelong glance at Simon. "Er, well, okay then, a coffee would be lovely."

After some small talk has ensued and we are finally sitting with coffee cups in hand, I bring up the subject of Hannah.

"Mary, we're here today to talk to you about a woman in the name of Hannah Greer." I wait for a second to see if I notice any response in her body language. Mary raises one eyelid.

Simon says, "Do you recall a Hannah Greer staying here?"

Mary opens her hands, palms upwards and says, "Well,

I'm not really supposed to talk about the women that stay here. One of the benefits of their visit is the knowledge that their details will be kept private and confidential..." She trails off.

I take a breath. "Mary," I begin. "I do appreciate that. However, in the case of a missing person investigation, you are required by law to disclose any information which may be relevant to the case."

At this stage Mary quickly replies. "I don't know where Hannah is."

I nod slowly and then say, "Okay, I appreciate that. However, have you ever met Hannah in the past?"

A look crosses her face, one, I think, of guilt. "Well yes," she discloses. "Yes, Hannah has stayed here in the past."

I throw a glance at Simon, one that says, I knew it!

"And," I continue, "how many times did Hannah stay here?"

Mary is now clasping her hands and rubbing them gently in her lap. "Two or three," she says. There's a thoughtful pause and then, "Yes, three times."

"Okay," I say. "And each time she returned to Kyle?"

Mary sighed. "Yes it happens all the time unfortunately. One apologetic word from the husband and they go back to him. The cycle continues all over again."

"I hear that's very common."

"It's very hard for them to break the cycle. It's like an addiction."

"Mary, did Kyle ever turn up here? Did he ever act abusive? Did he demand to see Hannah?"

She takes a deep breath. "He turned up yeah, several times. He wasn't abusive though. Quite the opposite in fact. Acted really charming and persuasive." Her face hardens. "But I saw through him. I knew what he was playing at."

"I see." There's another thoughtful pause. A grandfather clock ticks in the background. The sound is strangely soothing.

"And did Hannah ever report him, to your knowledge?"

She shrugs. "Wouldn't you be able to find that out from

your records?"

I clear my throat, embarrassed by her question. "Yes, we can. I just wondered if Hannah had ever said anything to you, if you ever had to phone the police for her on her behalf"

Mary shook her head. "No, Hannah would never do that. She was far too timid. She would never have reported him." She shrugged her shoulders. "She was too scared of what he'd do to her, if she dared report him."

I nod, building an image of Hannah in my head. This timid woman, who was clearly terrified of her husband.

"What's all this about?" Mary asks suddenly. "I've seen the news on Hannah. I know that she's missing. Do you think Kyle is responsible?"

I throw another glance at Simon, realising that I'm needing his back-up here. I'm not sure how much I want to tell Mary.

"Mary," Simon says. "We're doing a full investigation on Hannah. We're trying to find out everything we can about her in the hope that it will lead to her whereabouts."

"I wouldn't put it past him," Mary said. "If he's capable of abusing her, he's capable of…" She trails off, obviously not wanting to say aloud her thoughts on what Kyle could do.

"Did Hannah say anything to you Mary?" I ask. "Any plans she might have had for going away? Any plans for hiding from him?"

Mary shook her head resolutely. "No," she confirms. "The last time I saw Hannah, Kyle had convinced her to go out for dinner. He sweet-talked her over dinner and persuaded her to return home." She sighed. "The next morning she had packed her bag and he was coming to collect her." Mary took a sip of her coffee. "I said to her, I said, 'Hannah, don't do it. He'll never change. He'll be back to his old tricks in no time.' But she wouldn't listen to me. 'Mary', she said. 'He's different this time. He's changed. I can tell'." Mary shook her head despondently. "They all say the same thing. They all say, 'this time he'll be different'. It's soul destroying."

I give Mary a sympathetic smile. "I'm sure it is soul destroying, especially when you're trying to help them."

Mary gives me an appreciative smile in return.

"Mary," Simon interjects. "Do you have anything at all on paper to show that Hannah was here? A record of attendance? A fire safety record? A receipt of some kind?"

Mary looks hesitant, so Simon persists. "It's just that in the event of having to take Kyle to court, of having to prove evidence against him, it would really help if we had a record that Hannah stayed here."

I can almost see the cogs whirring in Mary's brain. The battle between wanting to help yet knowing that she swore Hannah to secrecy.

"Mary," I say, trying to convince her. "You told us yourself that it was unlikely Hannah would ever report him; that she'd be too scared to stand up to him. That's why it's up to me and you to stand up for her."

Mary took a deep breath. "You're right, I guess. Hold on, I'll go and check if I have anything." She takes a moment to slowly raise herself out of her comfy seat. "Ugh," she groans. "When you get to my age, you're better not sitting down because it's too hard to get up again."

I give a small laugh. "Oh, join the club. I'm the same. You want to see the shape of me trying to climb that hill!"

Mary laughs. "That hill is a nightmare. The bane of my life."

She leaves the room and Simon gives me a small wink. He mouths "nice work" and I feel my insides flutter with excitement.

***

Twenty minutes later we're leaving the women's aid, clutching all the paperwork we need.

I turn to Mary in the doorway. "Thank you so much for your help, and for all the good work that you do here."

She looks deeply touched by my comment. "Thank you dear. It was a pleasure to meet you. Good luck with the investigation. I'll be rooting for you that you find her."

"I'll let you know the moment I hear anything."

"Oh, please do," she croons.

And then we're off, careering back down the steep hill, which is much easier on the way down than on the way up.

"Nice work, Detective Kerry," Simon says, as we're walking along.

"Oh no," I say humbly, "It was a joint effort. We're a team."

"That's rubbish and you know it," Simon replies playfully. "You had her eating out of the palm of your hand. You're a natural, Kerry. You have a way with people."

I give a small "humph" in delighted response. "I wish I had a way with the men!" I find myself saying.

He 'tsk's'. "I'm sure you have them lining up to date you."

I feel my cheeks burn and hastily try to swipe my embarrassment away with a self-deprecating comment. "I should be so lucky."

At that moment the shrill tone of his mobile phone interrupts our conversation. He pulls his phone out of his pocket.

"Oh look," he says. "It's the missus." He presses a button and I hear him say, "Hello you. What's happening?"

There's a pause but I can hear a hysterical voice at the other end of the phone.

Then he says, "It's okay. Calm down. Don't worry,"

But the hysteria continues.

"We'll be straight over to you. And phone 999, okay?"

My ears prick up. "What's wrong?" I ask, concerned.

"It's Laura. There's been an accident. They're on the Ormeau Road. Let's drive there now."

"Of course," I reply, and I quicken my speed to match his.

He switches on the blues and twos and we speed over Belfast in the direction of Ormeau. On route he fills me in on what he knows so far.

"There's been a crash. She says it's not serious, but the back of the car is dented. The kids are fine, but Caitlin is crying. I think she was more worried about what I'd say about the car to be honest."

"But you can sort it out on insurance can't you?" I ask.

160

"Of course," he replies quickly. "As long as they're okay, I don't care about the sodding car."

I can tell from his tone that he's worried sick but trying not to show it. I decide to just sit quietly until we arrive at the destination. As we pull up I see her. She's holding one of the kids in her arms and the other is standing clutching on to her side. A selection of well-meaning/nosy passers-by have accumulated around her.

As soon as Simon gets out of the car he runs over to her, throwing his arms around her neck. I walk slowly towards them, keeping my distance and giving them a bit of space.

The kids are now hugging their daddy and they are all holding each other in a relieved embrace.

I walk slowly towards Laura. "Hey," I say softly. "Can I get you something from the café? A tea with sugar perhaps. It might help with the shock."

Laura looks at me, her face softening. "Oh, that's so very kind of you. I would love that actually."

"No worries," I smile, and I'm off, organising tea for her and soft drinks for the kids. I'm grateful to have a job to do to be honest. Otherwise I would feel awkward hanging around gawping at them.

I return and proffer the drinks in their direction.

"That's so very kind," Laura says gratefully. "Thank you so much."

"No problem," I say. "It's the least I could do. How are you holding up? That must have been such a shock?"

Laura lets out a breath. "It really was. It was all so fast. And I was just terrified that the kids..." The words catch in her mouth and a tear escapes down her face. Simon places a comforting arm around her.

"Sorry," she apologises to me. "I'm not normally like this, I swear." She takes a tissue and gives an embarrassed laugh through her snivels. "God, first time you meet me, and this is how I get on."

"Don't be silly," I say softly. "I'd be exactly the same. You've been through a really shocking event."

Laura gives a small laugh then turns to Simon and makes a

little joke. "You didn't tell me your work partner was such a looker."

Even though her comment is a joke, it's laden with jealousy and suspicion. It leaves me feeling stunned.

Simon pipes up. "A looker? Hardly. Mind you, she's wearing a bit of make-up today. That makes her look a bit less offensive."

I roll my eyes playfully to Laura. "That's the derogatory way he talks to me."

"Don't take it from him," she advises playfully.

"Okay, I won't." I smile.

Chapter Twenty-Eight

Julia

Hey xx

That is all his text says. *Hey.* I throw my phone back down on the sofa and pick up the remote control.

I can feel my insides fizzing with fury even though part of me wants to laugh when I think of how things have changed. If Kyle had sent me a text simply saying *hey* at the start, I would have felt a fizz of excitement. Now, it's a fizz of annoyance. At the start, it would have seemed like playful banter, a way to get in touch with me and test if I was interested in talking to him. Now, a simple *hey* just comes across as lazy, as though he couldn't be arsed to write anything longer than three letters. It was as if he expected me to do all the work, to write the flirty messages, to make all the effort.

I decide to ignore him. I can't be bothered to reply. No, change that, I don't want to reply. After that horrific night when he thrust himself on me, I decided that I would take a step back from him. Call it female intuition, but something just doesn't feel right. If he's capable of treating me like that, if there was a card about domestic violence in his home, if Hannah has gone missing, wasn't it all connected? Was Kyle some sort of abusive monster?

I shake my head. Perhaps I'm being paranoid. Perhaps I'm putting two and two together and making six. Perhaps it's all just a coincidence. Hannah's disappearance could be by some random sex attacker. The card for 'Arise' could have been anything – maybe Hannah had a friend staying there. And the weird sex, well, maybe he just has a kinky side.

But still, something doesn't feel right in my gut.

I can almost hear my friend Jinny's voice ringing in my ears. 'Julia, you're a nightmare,' she would say. 'The minute a guy shows he's interested in you, that there might be some commitment involved, you'll run a mile in the other direction. You're just terrified of being responsible to someone'.

She's right of course. That's why I'm always attracted to 'the bastards' I suppose. 'The bastards' never want commitment. They never expect you to stick around. They don't want any accountability from you. They are happy to just shag and go. All fun, no responsibility.

The 'nice guys' are always scarier. They give you flowers and chocolates and take you out for dinner. But in return they want you to meet their parents, they want to live together, they want commitment. And I know what commitment means. Commitment means falling in love, commitment means the risk of having your heart broken, commitment means fear.

'You're nuts', Jinny would tell me. 'Really properly nuts'.

And I would nod and agree with her. Because I knew I was. Because years of counselling had helped me to see that that was what was going on, deep down in the subconscious.

The funny thing is that the more I ignore Kyle, the more he pursues me. How typical! My phone beeps constantly, morning, noon and night.

He texts again, an hour later.

Hey xx

And again.

You out tonight? xx

God, it just shows you when you ignore them they up their effort from three letters to three words.

Then the following morning another one comes.

Morning babe, did you have a good night last night? xx

Again, I ignore him. I just want him to go away, to pretend like we've never met, to pretend that I never existed. I don't want to have to go through the hassle of breaking things off with him, when nothing has formally started in the first place.

But still the bloody texts persist. I get one at lunchtime.

Hey babe, I'm passing your way after work. Wondered if you're about for a drink?

Finally I reply.

Hey Kyle, sorry I've not been in touch. Something's come up – a family issue. I just need a bit of space at the moment. Sorry xx

It's my polite way of telling him that it's over. I hope he'll be able to read between the lines and realise that what I'm actually saying is, "*Kyle, I don't want to see you anymore. Stop texting me. Thanks and bye.*"

But no, he doesn't read it like that. Either because he's stupid or too stubborn to take no for an answer.

Aw babe, are you okay? Is there anything I can help with? Need a shoulder to cry on? Xx

I groan. Would he not ever get the message?

No, it's fine. I just need time to myself xx

In other words, '*please piss off*'.

His reply beeps in.

Okay babe, take it easy, speak soon xx

It feels as if the walls are closing in on me, as though I can't breathe. A cloud of claustrophobia engulfs me, making me feel like there isn't enough oxygen in the room. I need to get outside, to get some air.

When I arrive home that night, a huge bouquet is waiting on my doorstep. The note reads, '*Thinking of you. K xx*'

I take the flowers inside, the strong pungent stench of the lilies pervading each room. I hear a noise like the creaking of a step, and my heart jumps. Is he here? Has he let himself in? I tip-toe gingerly to the hallway and check up the stairs but there's nothing. I scold myself, realising that I must be hearing things. Then another noise makes me jump, but I realise it must be a noise emanating from the neighbour's house.

I decide to pour a glass of wine, hoping that it calms me down. But when I'm in the kitchen and cross to the cupboard to take out a glass, I swear I see a figure outside the window staring in at me. I jump, and the glass shatters to the ground.

"Fuck!" I exhale, but when I look back at the window the figure is gone, if it had even been there in the first place. Perhaps it had just been my own shadow in the windowpane.

I creep over the broken shards of glass and locate the dustpan and brush. Kneeling down, I sweep and scoop, trying to calm my breathing down. Jeez, why am I so spooked?

After I clear the glass I go around my apartment, closing all the blinds and curtains, and double-checking that the windows and doors are locked. I can't explain what has me so on edge. And yet, of course I knew what has me on edge - Kyle's behaviour the last time he was here, the aggressive nature in which he'd wanted to have sex, the disappearance of Hannah, and the fear that I could be next.

The thought settles anxiously in my gut, that I could be next. And yet here I am, living on my own, a ripe target.

I slurp back my wine, hoping that its soothing qualities would calm my mind. I switch on some mindless television, trying to fill my thoughts with a reality show full of z-list celebrities. And it works. Two bottles of wine and four hours of television later, I'm gently snoozing on the sofa.

I awake in the early hours of the morning, cold, and still lying on the sofa. I hurry up to bed, pulling my duvet around me. I check my phone. Thankfully no messages from Kyle. Perhaps he really is respecting my need for privacy. Perhaps I'm being too hard on him.

With a wry smile I think that if I really do want space from him, I should tell him that I want marriage and babies. That would surely make him run a mile.

I doze back off to sleep. When the alarm clock makes its shrill announcement later that morning I curse it.

Somehow I get through work without giving much thought to Kyle. The texts have stopped and he certainly seems to have gotten the message. Perhaps I should give him more credit than he's due. I'm sure it's not the first time a girl has ghosted him.

Several days passed and my phone remains silent. I begin to realise that I can relax. The whole Kyle saga is over. I will keep an eye on the news and hope for Hannah's reappearance, but at least I know that I am safe.

That is until the night someone grabs me out of nowhere when I'm walking home from work. A hand tightens around my arm and pulls me into an empty alleyway. A man presses himself up against me and a hand is covering my mouth so hard that I can only squirm in response.

Everything is so fast. The feeling of his body pressing hard into me. The smell of his hand against my nostrils. The pain shooting across my mouth as his hand pushes against my lips, my teeth.

"Ugh," I groan.

"Shut up, bitch," he hisses. "Don't make a sound."

At the same time I can feel his other hand grab me in between my legs, his fingers clamping against my crotch. "Don't make a sound or I'll hurt you," he hisses into my ear.

"What d'you want?" I try to say, behind his hand, but it comes out like "Wa oo wan?"

"You. I want you," he purrs, his fingers squeezing tighter on my crotch.

Even in that split second, even though it was all so fast, even though his face is masked, I know it's Kyle. I just know it.

Somehow my brain races to action. My knee swings involuntarily upwards, it crashes against his groin, I hear him squeal in pain, I use his second of weakness to push him backwards. I run. I run and I run and I run until I find the first doorway, a shop. I run inside. I scream "Police! I need police." And I run around behind the counter until I'm right beside the shopkeeper. The shopkeeper grabs the phone and I hear him saying "Police please." Bless that man. He asks no questions, he does what he is told. I lean on the counter, panting, fear and adrenaline pulsating through me. When the man gets off the phone he asks, "Are you okay, miss? What happened?"

So I tell him about the man appearing from nowhere, grabbing my crotch, putting his hand to my mouth, about me kicking him, about running.

Of course there was no sign of Kyle. He'd obviously run

off. He wasn't about to follow me into the shop.

The man got me a chair. "Here, sit," he orders. He beckons some woman over - maybe his wife. He says something in a different language, but I gather he is asking her to get me a cup of tea. Shortly after the tea arrives, laced with sugar. I sip it back gratefully. And finally the police arrive and ask questions, and take statements.

I know it was Kyle, I just know it. But of course I have no way to prove it and no desire to stay in my house alone. I call my friend Jinny. "Please can you come stay with me, just for a day or two?" And then I burst into tears. I tell her all about the man in the alleyway and the police.

"Give me ten minutes," she says. "I'll be straight over."

Chapter Twenty-Nine

Hannah

Kyle had come to collect me from the hospital that day. He looked like such a doting husband, I'll give him that. He fussed around me, making sure that my bag was packed, that I hadn't left anything behind. He took my arm and guided me gently out of the ward. He thanked the nurses profusely for all their hard work and dedication. He had even brought them a gift – a large tub of chocolates and a thank you card. They all cooed at him, like they were besotted. I'm sure they were feeling so jealous of my gorgeous, attentive husband. If only they knew.

In the elevator on the way down he was still fussing, saying that he was so glad to have me home again. I wondered if he said that for the benefit of the listening ears. A woman in a wheelchair, a man in his pyjamas, their faces drawn and unhappy, looking at us wistfully, as though we were so lucky.

I wondered when the act would slip. When would real Kyle come out to play? Perhaps it would happen when he got me into the car on my own. Perhaps the recriminations would start then. Perhaps he'd scold me for my cross words the other day.

But no recriminations came. In fact he was as good as gold, fussing over me, leading me to the sofa, putting a blanket over me, bringing me a cup of tea. He ordered a takeaway for us that night so I wouldn't have to cook. He poured me a glass of wine which I drank greedily even though I was still dosed up on painkillers. He was the ultimate attentive husband.

That's what made this roller coaster life with Kyle so

impossible. He'd raise your hopes, leading you up towards the sky, letting you see a beautiful view, reminding you of charismatic Kyle, the Kyle you fell in love with in the early dating days. And then all of a sudden, he'd turn, flip you over that loop and make you fall crashing towards the ground, terrified and hysterical, with just one cross word or one swift movement.

This time I knew to keep my guard up. I bided my time, counted the days. I had a plan. Guy and I had concocted it when he returned the next day. I knew I had to leave the hospital with Kyle; that I couldn't walk out the door with Guy. That would be too obvious, and the nurses would have to report to Kyle who I had left with. So I'd return home with Kyle and play along for a few days. And then later, when Kyle was at work and I had a bit of space, I'd just leave. I wouldn't pack a bag because Kyle might find it. Guy said that he'd put a few things together for me – pyjamas, toiletries. He was sure he could sneak some of Kate's that she hadn't used in a while.

I would just walk out the door, lock it behind me and walk away. That simple.

I wouldn't tell work because then Kyle might be able to trace me. I wouldn't tell anyone. It was our little secret. That's why Guy couldn't tell Kate either. She might be too tempted to confide in someone. That someone might confide in someone else. And before long, our secret would be out.

I texted Guy that day. "I'm on my way."

He texted back immediately. "Kate's still here. Hide in the shed at the back. I'll let you in as soon as she goes."

I crept behind the house. I peered in the window. No sign of anyone. I texted Guy.

I'm at the back, where's Kate?

She's in the shower, make a run for the shed now.

I ran, crept inside the shed and waited. It stank in there, a mixture of some god-awful weed killer or something. I sat on a large bag of soil. To be fair it was comfy enough. And I waited. And waited. And waited.

Jeez, how long does it take for a woman to have a shower

and get ready? Bloody forever, in Kate's case.

I pictured her straightening her long hair, applying her make-up, running a lipstick over her lips, pouting in the mirror. All the while, I sat on the soil, inhaling weed-killer fumes and dying for a wee.

I didn't text Guy again though. I didn't want her to see him checking his phone constantly and asking what the matter was.

Eventually I heard the click of the shed door. For a split second I feared Kate would have somehow needed something from the shed last minute, even though that was ridiculous.

But no, it was Guy, standing with a half-amused, half-apologetic expression.

"Sorry you had to wait so long," he said.

I welcomed the breath of fresh air that whipped inside the shed.

"All clear?" I asked, tentatively.

"Yeah, she's gone, But let's hurry you downstairs in case she forgets something and comes back."

He smuggled me into the basement. He had set out some goodies on the sofa for me – pyjamas, toiletries, some books.

"Did you get the tablets?" I asked.

He nodded. "Yeah, but don't be going overboard on them okay?"

I nodded, more to appease him than anything else.

"Okay, I better dash back upstairs. I don't want to be down here in case she returns."

"Sure, go," I said and I watched as he left the room, shutting and locking the door behind him.

I sat on the sofa and took a breath. After all the running around, the adrenalin, the fear, I was here, safe. Kyle would never find me.

***

<u>**Now**</u>

"Er yeah. I'm phoning about that missing person, Hannah

171

Greer. I've just found her," Kate's saying.

I've curled up into the foetal position on the sofa.

"Sorry Hannah," I hear Guy whisper.

I'm not annoyed at him. He has done the best he can. Hell, he's probably even put his relationship on the line for me. I know what Kyle would have done to me if I had hidden a man in the basement.

"I'm sorry too," Kate says when she comes off the phone. "But I have to tell the police. Can you imagine how much time they're spending trying to find you? Meanwhile we know you're here all along. We'd get in so much trouble."

"I know. I'm sorry. "

I am aware that my fingertips have crept into my mouth and I'm absentmindedly chewing on my nails. Fear engulfs me. Surely Kyle will find out where I am now.

"I'm not sure where to go now," I say. I think of that women's aid, the one I went to before. But I know that would be the first place Kyle would check. And then he would badger me to come home again.

I could run away to another town I supposed. But where would I stay? What job could I get? I had visions of me lying in some doorway like some helpless homeless person.

Kate looks at me. "Well, you'll still stay here of course!" she says.

I look up at her, surprise etched all over my face.

"Er... really?" I stutter. "But I thought you…."

She waves her hand away as though hitting a fly. "Oh, of course I want to tell the police of your whereabouts, but you're welcome to stay here as long as you like."

She looks around the basement room. "In a way, it's quite nice that my mum's old annex is being used for a good cause."

Then she brings a hand to her mouth, as though embarrassed. "I'm not saying you're a good cause, I'm saying…."

"It's fine," I interrupt her. I am a good cause, a charity case. I know that.

"In fact," Kate pipes up. "There's no reason for you to stay

172

down here. We have a spare bedroom. It even has an en-suite. You must move into it, I don't like the thought of you cooped up down here."

It's extremely kind but I want to tell her that I'm quite happy being cooped up down here, that it's the first time I have felt safe in a long time. But I don't want to seem ungrateful.

"Oh, that'll be the police," Guy says when the doorbell rings.

"We better go upstairs," Kate stands up.

And face the music, I think.

***

There are two police officers, one male and one female. They introduce themselves by their first names.

"I'm Kerry," the female officer says, holding out her hand to shake mine.

"I'm Hannah," I respond, terrified of what punishment I might receive.

"Oh, I know who you are," Kerry smiles. "We've been looking for you for quite some time, Hannah."

I squirm with embarrassment. "Sorry," I reply in a low voice.

"Just glad to see you alive and well," Kerry responds in a cheerful tone. "Could we sit down and ask you a few questions?"

I am ushered into the living-room. Guy comes too. Kate's gone off to the kitchen, busying herself by making tea and coffee.

It feels strange to sit in the living-room. I've never seen it before. My eyes wander around, taking in the modern décor, the tasteful furnishings. There's a huge orchid on a solid wood dining table and a large mirror hanging on the wall. A bookshelf holds photo-frames which cheerfully brag happy selfies of Guy and Kate. Huge circular candles are dotted around.

I realise I'm staring agog so I quickly turn my attention

back to the police officers.

There are endless questions. How long have I been down in the basement? Was I okay? Had Guy kidnapped me? Had Guy attacked me?

"Guy has done nothing wrong!" I blurt out angrily. "Nothing!"

Kerry throws a sidelong glance at the other officer, Simon.

"Er, Guy," Simon asks. "Would it be possible to speak to Hannah on her own for a bit?"

"Of course!" Guy jumps up to leave.

"He's done nothing wrong!" I persist. "It's all my fault!"

Kerry looks at me with a concerned expression. She obviously thinks this is some sort of Stockholm Syndrome thing; where the kidnapped person becomes attached to their kidnapper.

Kate returns with a tray of tea and biscuits. "Tea!" she announces cheerfully.

I take a cup and sip it back, then munch on a biscuit hungrily.

Kerry gives me a concerned look again. She must think that Guy has starved me downstairs. In actual fact I'm just starving after so much talking between me and Kate.

"Please don't make me leave," I urge. "Please don't make me go to the station. I'm terrified Kyle will find me."

Kerry throws another glance at Simon. She sits back in her chair, her legs folded, as though getting comfortable for a long conversation. "Hannah," she says. "Tell me about this Kyle. Start at the beginning. Why did you feel you had to run away from him?"

Chapter Thirty

Hannah

"We'd just like to give you an opportunity to tell your side of the story," a woman's voice is saying through the letterbox.

I shrink back, hiding my silhouette from the door.

"Please, Hannah. Everyone has been so worried about you. It'd be nice to give them a happy ending ."

I roll my eyes. This is the second journalist today that has tried to talk to me. I don't know how they've managed to track me down, but it terrifies me. If they can find me so easily it means Kyle can find me easily too.

"Hannah, I know you're in there," the voice persists.

I remain silent but retreat backwards until I can turn the corner and slink into another room, far removed from the front door. I want to go into the kitchen, but I can't. The journalist might poke her head through the window and catch me. I just want to go back down to the basement again. I felt safer down there. Every time I hear a noise or see a figure, I'm convinced it's Kyle.

I head upstairs to my new room. Kate has done it up for me – setting out towels and pyjamas. It's really very good of her. I can't imagine many other women being so accommodating about having another woman living in their home. But she's so open-hearted about it. I think she's enjoying the company to be honest. Last night we sat up all hours drinking wine and chatting. Guy had gone off to his study to write. She says he's writing like a demon at the moment, always tucked away at his keyboard, typing non-stop. She says it's best not to interrupt him when he gets into one of these zones. She says it won't last, that he has weeks or months of writing loads and then nothing. Then he'll be moping around the house lost and bored, so it's best to enjoy the busy periods while they last.

We had such a lovely chat. I told her everything, all about Kyle, right from the start. I didn't leave out anything. I think Kate has one of those faces. You feel you can tell her anything. She listens, really listens. She just sits there, her face nodding occasionally, not even interrupting with annoying *'aha's'* and *'yeahs'* like some people do. She should be a counsellor, she really should.

Anyway, Kate says I need to tell the police everything. She says I need to make a written statement and include absolutely everything that Kyle did. I told her I'd think about it. I don't know why I'm so reluctant.

I scroll through the latest local news and come across the heading, 'Missing Woman found in basement decides to stay in kidnapper's house.' I tut and roll my eyes. I can't imagine what this horrible publicity will do to Guy and Kate. But they tell me not to worry. They say that today's news will be tomorrow's fish and chip paper. I'm not so sure.

Kate and Guy are out tonight. They've gone to some writer event; I can't remember what it was exactly. It's funny, they apologised for going out as though I was their teenage daughter. They said, "We really wouldn't leave you on your own so soon, but we really can't get out of this one. It would be so good for Guy's career if he went."

I shooed them out and told them not to be so silly, that I'd be fine.

But now that I'm here, on my own, I don't feel so brave. I don't know if it's because this is an old house, but I can hear every single creak. It's eerie.

As soon as I'm convinced the journalist has gone, I creep downstairs to the kitchen. I quickly make myself a cheese sandwich and a cup of coffee. But just when I'm closing the fridge door, I jump. I swear I saw Kyle standing at the window looking in. My plate crashes to the ground and I cry out. Shards of the broken plate fly everywhere. I look back at the window again but there's no sign of him. I creep over the broken plate shards and rush to the window, peering out at either side. Still nothing.

In a panic I rush around the house, checking and double-checking every door and window, making sure that everything is locked. My breathing is fast and panicked.

I grab a dustpan and brush and quickly scoop up the broken shards. Then I grab the sandwich, shove it on a new plate and pick up the coffee cup. I also deposit the basement key in my pocket. I head down the stairs, back to my safe haven. I lock the door behind me and sit on the sofa. Taking huge breaths, I begin to calm down. I feel safer down here, I don't know why. Perhaps because it's quieter, and it feels more snug.

I eat my sandwich. I'm no longer hungry but I'm forcing myself to eat something.

But then, clear as day, I'm sure I hear a sound. I'm sure I can hear someone coming down the stairs. I immediately curl into a ball on the sofa, as though trying to protect myself. I instinctively reach for my phone and before I know it, I'm texting Guy and Kate, begging them to come home.

I'm thinking Kate will probably see her phone first, she's forever checking it.

Sure enough, she texts straight back.

Don't worry, we're on our way now xx

I breathe deeply, keeping my ears peeled. The creaking on the stairway seems to have stopped. Perhaps he's standing at the other side of the door. Perhaps he's about to break the door down at any moment. I'm suddenly thinking this is a stupid place to feel safe. I have no window to climb out of. I'm stuck here.

"Is it you out there?" I blurt out. "Kate and Guy are on their way right now. And I'm going to call the Police too." My fingers are shaking as I press '999' on my phone.

"Police, please," I'm saying, as loud as possible, in the hope that it deters him.

"Yes, there's been a break-in. He's in the house right now. I've locked myself in the basement. Please come now."

I hang up the call and listen intently. I'm waiting for the

sound of footsteps to retreat back up the stairs, but I can hear nothing. Perhaps he's trying to crawl up them quietly.

For some reason I begin counting in my head. One, two, three, four, five. I think that if I get to one hundred, Kate might be back by then. Twelve, thirteen, fourteen. I know what this counting thing is about. It's a way of trying to block out any other thoughts. If I can only concentrate on the numbers, I can't concentrate on anything else. Sixty, sixty-one, sixty-two. Come on Kate, come on Police. Ninety-nine, one hundred. Just keep counting. Maybe they'll arrive before two hundred.

One hundred and eighty-nine, one hundred and ninety.

I can hear Kate's voice as she clatters down the stairs.

"Hannah! Are you downstairs?"

"Yes! Yes! I'm here!" I cry in relief. I unlock the door and she flings through it, enveloping me in a hug.

"Are you okay?" she coos. "You poor thing! You must have been scared out of your mind!"

"I was terrified!" I cry, my head burrowing into her shoulder. "I swear, I thought I saw his face outside the window!"

Guy arrives through the door then, the police by his side.

"We shouldn't have left you on your own," Guy says apologetically. "It was too soon."

I shake my head. "No, I'm sorry. I'm so sorry for spoiling your evening."

Kate hugs me tighter and rubs her hand along my back in a comforting manner. "You didn't spoil it," she says. "In fact," she whispers conspiratorially, "You did us a favour. It was pretty boring."

I give an unattractive laughing snort as I try to wipe away my tears and blow my nose at the same time.

The same two officers are there from the other day; Simon and Kerry.

"There's no trace of anyone on the premises," Kerry assures me.

"I'm sorry. I could have sworn…" I say, embarrassed for wasting their time.

"She's obviously still massively traumatised." Kate says to the police. "I wonder, could we arrange some sort of protection order against Kyle, that he can't come in the vicinity of her?"

Kerry nods solemnly in my direction. "We should definitely look into that. We'd need to take statements and you'd need to speak to your solicitor."

In the past I would have shaken my head at this. I've never reported Kyle, not in all the years I've known him, no matter how many hospital visits, doctor visits, how many times I've been to a women's refuge, I've never once taken the matter to the Police. Kyle had always threatened that if I ever did it, he'd punish me so badly that I'd regret ever being alive. Well no more. For once in my life I was going to be strong. For once in my life I would fight back. Not because I was strong, but because I had Guy and Kate helping me.

I nodded. Just one small gesture but that one movement of the head was one of the strongest things I'd ever done.

"Yes," I said. "Yes, I'll make a statement."

Chapter Thirty-One

Julia

Thank God Jinny is staying with me for a few days. She sleeps in the bed next to mine and even though I can't sleep, it's a comfort having her here.

I'm sure that if Kyle is watching me, he's seen that I have a friend staying, and that his chances of breaking in are slim.

The police have been pleasant and kind enough, but I know there's nothing they can do. There is no evidence. I can't prove Kyle attacked me, so the Police can't just turn up and arrest him.

They do a quick scan of the alleyway though, using a torchlight to root around and see if he dropped anything, but I don't hold high hopes. I know Kyle is free to go and harass some other woman, and it sickens me.

And then I spot the front page of a local newspaper: *"Missing Woman found in basement decides to stay in kidnapper's house."*

I stop, my breath quickening. Hannah found? Trapped in a basement? Now staying on in the kidnapper's house?

My mind reels. Have I been wrong about Kyle all along? Perhaps it wasn't him who attacked me that night. Perhaps he had nothing to do with Hannah's disappearance.

After all, hadn't he spent all that time trekking around Cave Hill for her at the start? Why would he have done that if he was guilty?

My thoughts lapse briefly back to those early days, to that walk up Cave Hill with him, the spontaneous coffee we had in the café afterwards, the early flutter of …. Lust? Love?

I grab a copy of the newspaper, pay for it and quickly

scurry out of the shop.

Back at work that afternoon, I try so hard to concentrate but my mind keeps drifting to Kyle and Hannah. Part of me is even tempted to text him. To say something like, '*Great news about Hannah, I'm sure you're so relieved.*'

But the other part of me holds back. I'm still convinced about the attack. Even though his contact with me had been so brief, it had sounded like Kyle, felt like Kyle. Perhaps that was ridiculous or perhaps it was female intuition. Still, I couldn't exactly go to the Police and state my evidence as 'female intuition'.

Then there was the last time he had visited me, the aggressive way in which he'd had sex with me. No, I wouldn't text him. It would open a door that I was actually managing to close.

There's one person I'd want to text though if I had her number, Hannah. I want to tell her all about Kyle. I want to find out what she says about him. Would our stories match?

But that's another dead end. How could I get a letter to her? I don't know where this mysterious kidnapper's house is. I'm sure the press won't be allowed to release that for security reasons. Or would they? Maybe pictures would circulate of photographers camping outside. I'm sure I could figure out where she lives if I put my mind to it. Google Earth and a bit of snooping would help.

I just feel I have to *do something*. I can't just sit behind my desk, wondering. I have to get into action. I decide to draft a letter and then hopefully find some way of getting it to her.

Putting pen to paper, I begin.

Dear Hannah,

I'm sure you're getting loads of letters like this, but I wanted to write to say a couple of things. First of all, I'm so pleased that you've been found. We've all been worrying and following the news about you. I'm so glad for your safe return.

I've been following your journey from the start. In fact, I even did the walk up Cave Hill to try to find you, following

181

the #FindHannah campaign. How wrong we were climbing to the top when you were hidden in the bottom all along!

I do hope that you are safe and well and are recovering from this traumatic experience.

Hannah, there's something really important that I need to talk to you about. You see, I met Kyle on that walk to Cave Hill and I'm sorry to say, we became quite close. I don't want to burden you with any more stressful information at the moment but there are a few things I need to discuss with you about Kyle.

I'm not sure if you're going straight home to him. I heard something about you staying at the kidnapper's house. I'm wondering if it's for the reasons I'm thinking. Hannah, I'm sure you're being inundated with requests at the moment but I can assure you that I am 100% genuine. I'd be most grateful if you could spare me twenty minutes of your time. There's something I really need to talk to you about. It would help me massively if you could.

Kind regards,

Julia xx

***

I decide to give the letter to police officer Kerry. I ask if she would pass it on to Hannah for me. She promises that she will and says she thinks it would be a good idea. She says she will inform Hannah that I'm genuine.

All I can do is wait. Days roll by and no response from Hannah comes. I don't know if this is down to her being tired after her ordeal, or if she doesn't trust my intentions. Perhaps she doesn't want to hear anything bad about Kyle.

In the end I put it out of my mind. There's nothing else I can do. I've done my bit. I've written to her. I've extended a hand. I've tried. All I can do now is try to get on with the business of living.

Jinny has moved back into her own home. I can't expect her to stay with me any longer, it's not fair on her. But my sleep pattern is massively affected. I just can't rest at night.

Every noise I hear, I'm convinced it's Kyle coming back to attack me. I lay in bed succumbing to the insomnia and end up reading a book. When the alarm goes off in the morning, I drag myself out of bed. At work my eyelids feel so heavy. I could happily curl up under my desk and sleep if I can get away with it. One night I even stay in a cheap B&B just so I could be assured of a good night's sleep. The minute I close the door behind me I get into my pyjamas. I order room service, run a bath and then fall promptly asleep. It's bliss. But of course I can't make a habit of that, it would drain me financially.

I start to look at other flats, seriously considering a move. It seems drastic but I just can't relax in mine any more. Of course, I could go to all the hassle of moving house with all the headache and nightmare that it involves, simply to discover that Kyle has found out where I moved to. The thought both frightens me and makes me feel claustrophobic.

I begin to phone around estate agents though, arranging viewings, trying to do something rather than sit around fretting all day long.

My phone buzzes to life with missed calls and texts from pushy estate agents, all hoping to make the sale. I've learned to just let the calls click onto the answer phone. Once engaged with a sales advisor, I find it very hard to extricate myself from the call.

Taking a moment that evening after dinner to listen to the voicemail messages, my finger deletes one pushy advisor after the other until, that is, I stumble across a gentle spoken female's voice.

"Erm, Julia? Hi, it's Hannah here. I got your letter."

My ears prick up and I listen intently to her voice. Hannah.

"Er, yeah. I'd be available to have a talk with you about Kyle. Perhaps you could phone me back on this number and we can arrange something. Thanks."

Oh my god. She's finally responded. Hannah wants to talk.

***

"Thanks so much for agreeing to see me," I say, for what seems like the tenth time.

"It's fine," Hannah says quietly. "Kerry told me that it was okay to speak with you so…"

I nod eagerly, glad that Kerry has given her the comfort and reassurance she so obviously needs.

"I'm so glad you allowed me to come here," I gush, taking in the spacious kitchen. The kidnapper's home. How bizarre, I'm inside the kidnapper's home.

Hannah and I sit at the kitchen table, coffees in hand.

"So, what did you need to tell me?" Hannah asks. I start at the beginning, the walk up Cave Hill, the coffee, the early flirtation and dating. I give her an apologetic look. No woman likes to hear that her husband is having an affair. But Hannah doesn't flinch. She doesn't bat an eyelid. Either she is used to this behaviour from him or she doesn't care anymore.

And then I tell her about the Police searching his house, his attitude, about finding the card with the name 'Arise' across it. I study her face carefully as I say this. I can see the look of recognition flickering across her eyes, her memory that she had set the card in there.

I tell her about visiting the women's aid, about speaking to a woman called Mary, about asking her tons of questions, about Mary telling me nothing.

I see a smile creep at the edges of Hannah's lips, a recognition that Mary had protected her anonymity.

And then I tell her about Kyle being aggressive sexually, about how much it frightened me, about how I decided to take a step back from him after that.

And finally I tell her about the attack, about how I can't prove that it was Kyle, but how I suspect that it was him.

Hannah listens through all of this, not interrupting once.

Eventually, when I'm finished and a silence hangs in the air, I shrug my shoulders.

"Well, that's it." I say. "That's all I had to tell you."

I see that her eyes are glistening with tears. "I'm so sorry.

I'm so sorry that you had to go through all that."

She leans over, puts her arms around me and embraces me tightly. "I'm so sorry. I'm so, so, sorry."

I feel tears spring to my eyes then too. The fact that she is comforting me, the fact that she believes me.

She wipes the tears away from the corners of her eyes and blows her nose. "I'm so sorry because if I had stood up to him in the first place you wouldn't have had to go through all this. If I had reported him, if I had told the Police, if I hadn't just have run away, then you would never have had to go through all of this."

I hug her back tightly. "Oh no, no, no. Don't you go blaming yourself, Hannah," I say. "This is not your fault. It's his fault. It's all his fault."

She wipes her eyes. "I know, but still, I should have said something."

I clasp her hands in mine. "But it's not too late," I urge. "We can both say something. Now. Both of us can make statements. Both of us can report him so that he doesn't do this to anyone else. It stops here, okay?"

I look into her eyes, so frightened and vulnerable.

She nods back. "Yes," she agrees. "Yes, it stops here."

Chapter Thirty-Two

Kerry

"I'm telling you Kerry, it's a waste of time." Simon is sitting at his desk opposite me, about to tuck into a bacon sandwich.

"But how can you say that? We now have a statement from Julia and a statement from Hannah. Surely I could bring him in here for an interrogation."

Simon shrugs his shoulders. "You could, but he'll deny it."

I stare at him, exasperated. "I don't believe you," I say. "After all the work we've done on this case, are you willing to just drop it now?"

"Kerry, Hannah has been found, she's safe and well. That's all we were ever concerned about. This is a simple domestic issue. It's now up to Hannah if she wants to follow this up with solicitors and get a protection order from him. There's nothing we can do."

My mouth hangs open. "I don't understand it. Why are you being like this? We have all the evidence we need. Statements from the two women, evidence from 'Arise' that Hannah stayed there, and more! Why can't I bring him in for questioning?"

"Okay, okay! Bring him in. But I'm just warning you, he won't admit to anything. I'm just letting you know in advance that it'll be a waste of time."

I roll my eyes. "God, what's got into you this morning?" I say, in what I hope comes across as light banter. "Anyone would think you had PMT or something."

Simon looks at me and tuts. "Cheeky," he says. He drains the rest of his coffee and sets his cup back on his desk. "Okay then, if you must know, Laura gave me a right earful last night."

I raise my eyebrows, glad that no-one else is in the office so that he'll continue with his confession.

He sighs. "It seems that.... well, it seems that she has a problem with me working alongside you." He finishes the sentence with a flourish, as though knowing that it will shock me.

"Me? Why?"

He shrugs his shoulders. "Oh I don't know. Something about you being a female and having a vagina probably."

I wince. "Ugh. "

"Seems she wants me to work with some balding, fat, middle-aged man, just so that she can feel secure in herself."

I give him a sympathetic look. "Aww, I kind of get her point,"

He raises his eyebrows. "You do? Why?"

I sigh. "She's insecure because she loves you."

"It's bloody annoying is what it is," he huffs.

"Oh come on," I tease. "How would you like it if she was working alongside some bloke all day long?"

"I wouldn't care," he announces bravely.

"You wouldn't care," I repeat.

"Nope! I would be secure in my own skin to know that if she was married to me, she must love me."

"Yeah right," I tease.

"It's true!" he argues. "Anyway, I told her that you're a pain in the arse and one woman in my life is bad enough, never mind two."

"You cheeky bastard! You didn't say that?"

"I did!"

"Well I hope it appeased her."

"Momentarily. She'll probably not mention you again for...oh, at least forty-eight hours."

I shake my head. "But this is crazy. Laura is gorgeous. She's way beyond my league."

"I know. That's what I said."

"Are you wanting me to partner up with someone else or what?"

"God no. And miss taking the piss out of you every day? You must be joking."

"Well, maybe I need to meet this Laura again, hang out with her for a bit, let her see that there's nothing going on."

"You reckon?"

"Yeah, why don't we all go out to dinner or something?"

"Hmmm," he muses. "I don't know. I'll see."

And then I realise something. There's nothing, absolutely nothing between Simon and me. What I thought at first was attraction isn't that. Admiration for him, yes, respect for how good he is at his job, yes. Trying to impress him and show him that I'm good at my job, definitely. But wanting to pinch his wife off him and take him away from his kids, no. I'm sure that if he had turned around at that instant and confessed his secret admiration for me, I would have run a mile. Firstly, if we were to get together romantically, I could kiss goodbye to working in this station, and that's the last thing I'd want to do. Secondly, after all the suffering women I'd witnessed lately, the last thing I'd want is to be responsible for further suffering.

"Okay, well I'm going to go ahead and call Kyle in for questioning. I'm hoping I can prove you wrong."

Simon stands up to leave the office. "I sincerely hope you can prove me wrong Kerry. I'll be watching in Suite C2."

"Okey-dokes!" I pipe up. "Oh, and Simon?"

"Yup?" he burls around.

"Take Laura out for dinner. Buy her some flowers. Give her a bit of attention. That's all she's secretly asking for," I say in a low voice.

"Okay, Miss Agony Aunt," he groans, and he's off.

***

"Thank you for coming in today, Kyle," I say as I lead him into suite C1.

"That's alright," he chirps. He has no idea why he has been brought in. All I said on the phone was that I needed to ask him a few questions to help me with the case of Hannah's kidnapping. As far as he knows, he's here to be helpful.

"Would you like a coffee or anything? Some water?" I ask.

"Er... a coffee would be great yeah. Milk, two sugars."

"No problem." I stand up and head towards the door, poking my head out and asking an assistant to help.

A bit of small talk ensues until we have coffees in hand.

"Now, Kyle, as I said on the phone, I just have a few questions I need to ask you. There are a few loose ends we need to tie up. Hopefully you'll be able to help with our investigation."

"Sure, no problem," he agrees.

"I will warn you that this discussion is being recorded both audibly and visually but that is standard procedure so nothing to worry about."

"Sure." He sips his coffee, his manner relaxed.

"Now, obviously we are all very happy that Hannah has been found..."

"Yeah, it's a relief," he agrees.

"But I understand that all the while she has been staying with friends, Kate and Guy. Is that right?"

"Yeah," Kyle says. "Seems a terrible waste of police time," he admits. "I'm really sorry about that."

"It's not your fault. You weren't to know."

He nods, appeased by my acknowledgement.

"Why do you think she didn't say anything?" I ask.

He shrugs. "Oh you know how it is. All couples have arguments at times. Sometimes one wants a bit of space to themselves. There's a simple domestic dispute. It should never have turned into a full-scale missing persons."

"Why do you think she didn't just say that to you?"

He shrugs. "I guess she didn't want me to know where she was. I guess she wanted to make sure she'd have space to herself." I can see that he's squirming slightly. He doesn't like these questions.

"Surely she would know that you would just give her that space," I probe.

"Well yeah, of course I would," he responds.

"Kyle..." I continue. "Are you willing to give us any

189

details that we might need today? Is there any evidence that we can use to prove that you are not responsible for her disappearance?"

"What kind of evidence? Of course you know I'm not responsible ."

"Well yes, obviously," I say. "But for the purposes of paperwork and closing off this case, it would be good to cross a few ts and tick a few boxes."

He shrugs. "Well, whatever."

"Okay, great," I say decisively. "So all I'll need is a sample of your DNA and a copy of your footprints. My assistant will take those from you in a separate room. Then we'll meet back here. Would you like anything to cat or drink? I can get you a cheese toastie or some more coffee."

"Er... some more coffee would be great " he agrees.

"Okay, see you soon Kyle," I smile sweetly, leading him to the door. "I'll get that coffee for you and thanks again for your time. See you in a minute."

He's out the door and being led along to a separate room to give evidence before he knows where he is.

***

"Kyle, thanks again for that. This will really help to close off the case," I say, welcoming him back.

He settles down at the table and takes a tentative sip of his coffee.

"Kyle..." I begin. "I understand that you became acquainted with Julia Matthews just after the disappearance of your wife."

"Er, well yeah. She helped with the Find Hannah campaign."

"Hmm hmm. And did this friendship become... romantic?" I ask.

He shrugs. "I don't see what that has to do with anything."

"Quite a lot, it seems Kyle." I say, about to issue my first blow. "We have a statement from a Ms Julia Matthews about a sexual attack that you made on her."

190

"What? That's bollocks! It was consenting sex."

"Not according to Julia," I say. "She came to the station the following morning to report the assault. A physical examination was made on her, and the DNA is comparative with that which you have just given us."

"That's because it was consenting sex!" he persists.

"Not according to Julia," I repeat. "She didn't take any of your calls for quite some time after that in order to avoid you."

Kyle shrugs. "I thought she had just lost interest or something."

"Then an attack took place," I say, referring to my notes, "on the night of Thursday 8th November." I look at him, waiting to see a look of recognition cross his face.

"And what? That has nothing to do with me!"

"Is that right? That's interesting, Kyle, because some footprints were taken that night from our detectives and the samples that you have given us today are a complete match." I hold up two pieces of paper showing identical footprints.

His face clouds over with anger and indignation. "It can't be!" he persists. "This is a set-up!"

"Kyle…" I say. "Of course it's not a set-up. You know and I know that you were there on the night that Julia was attacked and that you are to blame."

He stares at the two pieces of paper, studying them endlessly. I'm aware that he's buying time, trying to come up with some explanation. I let him squirm.

"Kyle," I whisper. "What are we gonna do?"

He shakes his head as though trying to magic away the evidence.

"Well, even if I happened to be walking down that alleyway that night, what does that have to do with anything?"

I look at him, a knowing smile spreads across my face. "That's interesting, Kyle, that you knew that Julia was attacked in an alleyway."

He flummoxes, aware that he's given himself away. "I'm assuming it was an alleyway, that's all!"

"Hmm, hmm," I nod, showing him with my body language that I don't believe him.

"You said earlier!" he insisted. "You said that she was attacked in an alleyway."

"No I didn't Kyle," I purr softly. "I didn't mention an alleyway."

He shrugs. "Well, whatever. What does this have to do with anything?"

I pick up my papers again. "We also have some documentation here that we have recovered from Hannah's behalf. Reports from her doctor about injuries that she has sustained in the past and reports from her hospital about more severe injuries."

"And what?" he says, his tone becoming more aggressive as our chat continues. "She's accident-prone! She'll tell you that herself. She's always bumping into things or falling. It's nothing to do with me."

"Is that right? Well not according to Hannah. She has given us a very full and detailed statement of all the abuse she has suffered under your hands."

"She did what?" he fumes.

"Yes, she told us everything Kyle," I say. "Including the time you pushed her down the stairs and she lost the baby."

"She slipped!" he exclaims. "She was drinking wine, even when pregnant with our baby! She was drinking wine and slipped!"

"Kyle," I say, my voice levelled and calm. "We have statements from Julia and Hannah, doctor and hospital reports, evidence that Hannah resided in a women's refuge on several occasions and evidence that you attacked Julia. You're an intelligent man. Please don't deny that all this adds up to support the reason why Hannah chose to hide herself away from you?"

What would it take for him to admit that he was in the wrong?

Silent treatment descends upon him. His lips clench shut and he refuses to say anything.

"Kyle," I say. "I can see that your mind is racing. What

can I help you with? What is it that you're struggling with?"

Finally he opens his mouth. "Well what would happen if I was charged?"

"Well obviously we would have to take a statement from you and those statements would be handed on to solicitors. Julia and Hannah would arrange to have a protection order against you, so that you can't come in a certain vicinity of them. Then there would be a court order and it would be up for the judge to decide."

Kyle's mind was racing, I could tell. "Decide what?" he asks.

"Well, the judge would decide whether it would remain a simple protection order, or grow into a fine, or, in some cases, even a jail term."

"Jail?" Kyle croaks. "Really?"

"In some cases, yes," I say. "The thing that would help you, Kyle, is being honest today. If you admit to what you did, then your punishment would be less severe. However if you continue to deny it, I'm afraid it would mean that the Judge would have less compassion for you. I may remind you Kyle," I add, "that this entire conversation is being recorded both visually and audibly so the Judge will be watching this."

Kyle's squirms uncomfortably in his chair. "So what happens now?"

"Just tell me the truth Kyle," I say.

A deafening silence hangs in the air while Kyle is obviously mulling all of this over in his troubled mind. Finally he adjusts himself in his chair and opens his mouth to speak.

"Okay, where do I start?" he asks.

I take a huge breath of relief and smile in appreciation of his honesty.

"Just start at the beginning Kyle."

Chapter Thirty-Three

Kerry

"Just start at the beginning," I say to Kyle, as he sits across from me, head in his hands.

He sighs. "With Hannah you mean?"

"Yes, with Hannah," I say. I take a sip of my coffee.

"Well it all started out great with Hannah. We just clicked, you know?"

I nod.

"And, well, I just fell in love with her so quickly. We were inseparable."

I nod again, remaining silent, giving him the space to continue.

"And so I proposed pretty quickly. And she said yes. And everything was fine, until we went on honeymoon that is." He sighed, took a sip of his coffee and continued.

"I thought she was pretty flirtatious with some guy at the hotel – one of the workers. I thought I knew her – I thought I trusted her - until I saw the way she was getting on. I thought, 'that's not my Hannah. She would never flirt with someone in front of my face'. But it turns out, she would."

Some silence descends as he recalls the event and I remain quiet, keeping eye-contact with him.

"So I kind of made it clear I wasn't happy with her behaviour. I mean, I didn't hit her or anything, but she knew by my frosty attitude that she shouldn't act like that again. And she didn't, to be fair."

"But then," he went on, "she started banging on about the children thing. I mean, we were only married five minutes and she started saying that she wanted me to go for tests, to see what my fertility was like. I was mortified. It seemed so insulting. I wanted to say to her, 'hold on Hannah, did you marry me for me, or did you marry me for my sperm?'" He shook his head, the memory of the incident clear in his mind.

I wanted to roll my eyes at Kyle. I wanted to say 'Jeez, that's ridiculous'. But I remained quiet, unmoving. It was important to make it seem like I was a listening ear, a counsellor, otherwise I would never have gotten anything out of him.

"I didn't talk to her about it though," he shrugged. "I think I stomped off, made it apparent that the subject was off the table. But that's what men do, don't they? They clam up about stuff."

I wanted to shake my head and disagree with him, but I took a sip of my coffee instead.

"And I remember feeling this sense of being emasculated. It was as if I wasn't good enough for her, as if my sperm wasn't working fast enough for her … And I remember, just kind of acting out on that, as though I kind of wanted to show her who was boss. I wanted to show her that actually I could be a man. I could be assertive and powerful and in control and…"

He hung his head.

"I remember getting arsey about things, about the cleaning not being good enough, silly things. It was almost as though I was wanting to show her that I was masculine. It's silly, I know. And then I'd feel guilty, so I'd try to make it up to her, pamper her, give her foot massages, bring her breakfast in bed, stuff like that. Ways to show her I was sorry. I never said sorry of course, I was too proud for that. But I wanted to do something."

"And then one day I made the mistake of going through her phone. I don't know what I was looking for exactly. Call it intuition, I dunno. But I found messages from this Guy fella." He gave a sarcastic chuckle at this point. "Actually, it's the fella that she has decided to live with currently, so, I mean, perhaps my suspicions weren't all that ridiculous. Perhaps I knew. I dunno."

"Anyway, I confronted her about Guy, and she got all defensive, so I just knew there must be something going on. And I read the text and it was all about him wanting to take her out for coffee. And, I mean, Hannah is so naïve. She really doesn't think that when a guy says 'coffee', he actually means 'sex'. And I just... flared up. I just couldn't bear the thought of her with another man... and I just lost it."

"What do you mean by lost it, Kyle?"

"Well, I grabbed her by the throat," he said in that calm, quiet voice.

I nodded, even though it felt like bile was rising in my throat. On the one hand I was disgusted at him, but on the other I knew that I had to remain calm and detached, otherwise he would clam up. I could picture Simon, on the other side of the window, taking notes, giving a triumphant thumbs up that Kyle was confessing.

"And what happened then?" I asked, quietly.

"Well, I left the house and gave myself space to calm down. And I did calm down. And when I returned it was never discussed." He took a large breath. "And then she got pregnant. And it was wonderful. And we were so happy."

He continued. "But then I couldn't believe it. After all her determination to get pregnant, I actually found out that she was drinking on the sly! She was pregnant with our child and pouring alcohol into her belly. I couldn't believe she could be so stupid or so selfish. How dare she risk the health of our child?"

"And how did you discover this, Kyle? How did you find that out?"

He shrugged. "Oh, I came across bottles everywhere. There were bottles hidden in the laundry basket, bottles hidden under the mattress, bottles hidden in the hot press. It was pathetic." His lip curled in disdain.

"And cameras?" I probed. "Did you set up hidden cameras to watch her?"

"Those cameras were there for security in case we were ever broken into, so that I'd have evidence for the Police!"

I nodded even though I didn't believe him. God he was

good, I thought. No wonder Hannah found it so difficult to release himself from his clutches. He had an answer for everything. Somehow he managed to make himself sound like the victim in all of this.

"I suggested she see a counsellor," he went on. "I thought she needed to look at why she was drinking so much. I paid for counselling sessions for her and everything. I did try my best, you know?"

"Why do you think she was drinking so much Kyle?" I asked. How silly of me to ask him. Of course he wouldn't say something like 'because she was so unhappy with me. Because she felt like she was constantly walking on eggshells'.

"Oh god knows," Kyle shrugged. "Paranoia, anxiety, I don't know." He sips his coffee. "Anyway she wasn't even grateful that I had paid for the sessions for her. She seemed to take it as a hardship or an insult, rather than me genuinely trying to help."

I sipped my coffee and waited for him to continue.

"And then one day she just upped and left. She disappeared off to some women's aid. I couldn't believe it. Eventually I found her. I begged her to come back. And she did. But every once in a while, she'd just disappear off there again. It was as if she was punishing me, as if she was saying, 'you better bloody be in a good mood every day or I'm going to leave and take our unborn baby with me.'"

I listened, fascinated by how much denial Kyle was in. "And had you lifted your hand to her again in the meantime, Kyle? I can't imagine a women's aid would let her stay unless there was a reason."

He rolled his eyes. "Oh, we'd had a few arguments here and there, but that's what every couple does, isn't it? Every couple has their squabbles."

I paused. "Squabbles Kyle, yes. But not aggressive fights which lead to hospital visits and women's aids."

I could see redness creeping up Kyle's neck. Clearly my questioning was angering him. The fact that I was trying to argue Hannah's corner had left him annoyed.

"Well hold on a minute," he interjected. "How would you feel if you knew that your partner had been stealing money off you? How would you feel if you weren't even sure if the baby was actually yours? You'd get a bit irritable too, wouldn't you?"

I took a long slow breath. "I think that money which goes towards joint living expenses for food is understandable. I think that getting a bit irritable so that you push her down the stairs and she loses the baby is another."

Kyle's face fumes with anger. "I didn't push her!" he protests loudly. "She tripped! She had been drinking and she tripped!"

I shake my head. "No, Kyle. We have reports from the hospital and they found no traces of alcohol in her system that evening. They believe that the fall was so aggressive that it would have had to be a push rather than a simple trip."

He tuts. "Well I don't know then. Unless my hand accidentally brushed against her or something then, I don't know."

"Your hand might have accidentally brushed against her?" I repeated.

"Maybe," he shrugs.

"Accidentally brushed against her so forcefully that she lost the baby?" I repeat again.

"I don't know," he says, flummoxed.

"And then what happened?"

He shrugs. "And then I go to visit her in the hospital. She seems okay. She comes home again. And then she disappears. Again."

"So did you try the women's aid again?"

"Yeah, I did, but she wasn't there. Or at least, that's what they were telling me. So that's when I phoned about the missing persons. Have you any idea how frustrating it is to be with someone who keeps disappearing back and forth like a bloody yoyo?"

"Well, she had just lost the baby, Kyle."

He blanches, unable to reply.

"Well how would you like it if she ran off to live with the

man that she probably fancies, not telling anyone where she was going?"

"This is not about me, Kyle. This is about you. You and Hannah."

He puts his head in his hands then, remaining silent. He really was playing the victim big style, it was unbelievable.

"So what now?" He shrugs.

I take a breath. "Well, I'll pass the recordings of this conversation on to Hannah's solicitors and they will take it from here. I'll say again that I'm very grateful for your honesty today."

He nods and then gives me a smile which makes me feel both sick and queasy.

Standing up, I shake his hand. "Thanks for coming in, Kyle. We'll be in touch."

Chapter Thirty-Four

Kate

"Hannah." I knock on her door gently. "Breakfast is ready."

"Oh thanks!" I hear her call. "I'll be down in a second!"

I pad downstairs to the kitchen and head towards the coffee machine. Guy is already sitting at the breakfast bar, coffee in one hand, paper in the other.

"Wow! That smells amazing!" I hear Hannah say as she approaches the kitchen.

I look up and give her a warm smile. I notice that she has her hair piled back in a high ponytail and her face looks fresh and well rested.

"Sleep well?" I ask, smiling.

"I did actually," she replies.

I'm not sure if she's just saying that to make me feel better. I know for a fact that she hasn't been sleeping. I can hear her getting up to go to the loo several times throughout the night but I say nothing. I'm sure it will take time for her to be able to relax enough to sleep.

Spooning bacon, eggs and mushrooms onto three plates, I listen to Guy and Hannah who have settled into morning small talk.

I must admit I'm enjoying having Hannah around more than I thought I would.

Partly, it's because I enjoy our late night girlie chats. When Guy is tucked away in his study writing, Hannah and I sprawl out on the sofa, sharing a bottle of wine and putting the world to rights.

Some people would find it strange to have another woman living in their home, but it's not like that with Hannah. In fact, prior to Hannah, Guy and I struggled to make conversation at times. Looking back I realise that it's because he was stressed. He had this huge secret about Hannah that he felt he couldn't tell me. No wonder he struggled to make conversation. He was so worried he would say something he'd regret.

But now he's changed. It's as if he's relieved that the secret is out. And I know for a fact that he's relieved by my acceptance of it. He said as much to me last night. We were snuggled up in bed, and he lay facing me.

"Kate?"

"Hmm?"

"Thank you."

"Thanks for what?" I asked quizzically.

"For how you're being about the Hannah thing. For how accepting you're being. For how you're allowing her to stay here."

He looked at me with those big deep brown eyes of his and I could feel my heart melt a little.

"Aww, of course!" I replied. "It's the least I can do. That poor woman has been through so much."

"She has," he agreed.

"I only wish that you'd felt like you could have confided in me from day one. I only wish you didn't feel you had to hide a secret from me."

"I know, I'm sorry," he said. "No more secrets from here on, okay?"

"Definitely," I agreed. "No more secrets."

"And you've been so good to her," he continued. "I'm sure any other woman would have told her to move out asap."

"God no!" I declare. "And then where would she go? She'd be a nervous wreck. She can't even settle in the house if we're not here."

"I know. But hopefully in time that will ease. I really think she needs some counselling or something to help her deal with all this."

"Definitely. But how do we suggest that to her without it seeming like an insult? We can't exactly say, 'Oye Hannah, you need a counsellor'. She'll take it as 'Oye Hannah, you're nuts'."

Guy smiled at me. "I'll have a word with her."

"Do," I said. I picked my book up as though that was the discussion over.

But I could feel Guy still looking at me. I twisted my head towards him. "What?" I smiled.

He gave me one of his wistful smiles. "Nothing."

I knew what was going through his mind. I had lived with him for long enough now to be able to read his facial expressions. This was the face he gave me when he was about to pop the question.

"Go on, say it." I prompted. Was I really encouraging him to propose to me again? Did I feel differently about the marriage thing now?

I don't know, but I had noticed some sort of shift in our relationship since Hannah came along. I'm not sure why.

Perhaps it was the fact that I was impressed by Guy's character. Anyone who would go so far out of their way to try to help someone in distress was clearly an honourable person.

The fact that he hadn't taken advantage of her vulnerability also didn't go unnoticed by me.

And there was something different about him now. He seemed more relaxed. He tucked himself away in his study writing like a demon. He seemed more driven, more passionate about his dreams.

And if I was honest with myself, I had changed too. Hannah had brought something out in me that I didn't know was there, a desire to help someone, a sort of maternal instinct. I liked cooking for her. I liked to see her relaxing. After all the trauma she'd been through, I loved to see her starting to unfurl, like a cat out-stretching her paws. And, of course, it had helped my relationship with Guy. It seemed as though we had more to talk about now - a common goal, the goal of helping Hannah.

"Go on, say it." *Ask me,* I urged. *I'm okay if you ask me.*

But his wistful smile had fallen and I could almost see the cogs turning in his brain. I could see his reticence to propose after the last time where I had flung the proposal back in his face. I cringed inwardly at the memory.

He leaned over and planted a kiss on my lips. "Goodnight honey," he'd said eventually. "I love you."

And I knew that he'd never ask me again.

***

"Kate!" Guy exclaimed, bouncing into the kitchen. "You'll never believe this."

"What?" I asked, looking up from the coffee machine, the suspense killing me.

"I got an email back from the publishers. They love the book!"

"What?" I squealed. "You're kidding!" My face had broken out in a huge grin.

"I'm not kidding," he replied excitedly. "I'll show you the email." He lifts up his laptop and sets it on the breakfast bar. "Look." He guides my eyes towards his latest email entitled, "Re: Submission."

My eyes scan through the email, the words spinning around in my excitement to take it all in.

Guy,

Many thanks for the submission of your full manuscript as per our previous emails.

We would be very interested in publishing your novel and we attach herewith the terms and conditions of contract which we would ask you to read and sign.....

"Oh my God!" I squeal. "Oh Guy! That's amazing!"

I can see the tears of relief, tears of gratitude, tears of realisation in his eyes that all his months and years of hard work and determination have finally paid off.

I lean over and grab him in the tightest hug I've ever given him in my life.

"Oh Guy, I'm so proud of you honey. I'm so proud."

I can see the tears have escaped from his eyelids now and are coursing down his cheeks.

"They're good tears!" he protests. "Happy tears!" He lets

out a chuckle and I laugh too. The tears are falling down my face now too and I reach over and grab some tissues from the counter and we're standing there, laughing and crying and wiping our faces at the same time.

"Go and tell Hannah!" I laugh. "And let's have a celebration tonight!" I cry. "We're opening that champagne!"

He grins, places another kiss on my lips, and runs off to tell Hannah his good news.

Chapter Thirty-Five

Kerry

"Good evening ladies and gentleman," a male voice boomed over the loudspeaker. "Welcome to the annual award ceremony for the Northern Ireland Police Force."

A din of voices continued chatting until loudspeaker man said, "Can I have your attention please? Quiet."

The din of voices hushed to a quiet as all eyes turned towards the speaker at the front of the marquee. Dressed in suit and bow-tie, he held a piece of paper in front of him and read from a script.

"It is my pleasure to announce to you the winners of the awards in the following categories…"

As he prattled on, I looked around the marquee with interest. How strange it was to see all my fellow colleagues suited and booted in fancy tuxedos and flowing gowns rather than our normal uniformed attire. For myself, I had hired a black evening dress with long sleeved black gloves and a large ornamental ring on my finger. My hair had been swept into an up-do with tendrils falling down on each side. It felt like such a lovely change to be dressed up and glamorous, rather than sitting in trousers and boots every day.

On my table were Barry, Peter, Simon and his wife Laura. Laura looked spectacular. She was wearing a figure-hugging red satin dress which showed off every inch of her curvy figure.

"And the award for the best newcomer goes to…." the man's voice interrupted my reverie. "Kerry Lawlor!"

I gasped. Simon, Laura and the others on my table all turned to face me in surprise.

"Go get 'em Kerry!" I heard Simon say, and "That's fantastic Kerry!" Laura agreed.

"Go up! Go up!" Simon encouraged.

"Oh my god!" I said, getting to my feet and hoping that the jelly feeling would go away so that I could at least make it to the stage without fainting.

A ripple of applause spread out among the room as I made the walk towards the podium. How proud would my mum be if she could see this? I battled not to let any tears fall to my cheeks as I finally reached the podium.

"Congratulations Kerry," the man said, his voice soft and warm. He shook my hand and then proffered the award in my direction. "Can you say a few words?"

I took the award in my hand and turned to face the sea of people in front of me. Spotlights shining into my eyes made it difficult to see but I tried my best to say a few words.

"Goodness me!" I said, my voice breathy with excitement. "I really wasn't expecting this at all!" I held the award with pride and joked. "When this announcement was being made, I was just looking around the room noticing how fantastic everyone looked with their fancy clothes on!"

A ripple of laughter spread throughout the room.

"Well," I continued. "I'm not going to do a Gywneth Paltrow, I promise. I will just say that I'm utterly delighted to receive this award and it's been an absolute joy to work here. I'd like to thank Simon and the team for putting up with me. Hope you all have a fantastic night!" I held the award triumphantly and heard a few resounding cheers from the crowd. I then concentrated very hard on getting off the podium and back to my chair in one fell swoop.

Back in my seat, my knees still quivering like jelly, Laura turned to me and placed a hand on mine.

"Congratulations, Kerry, that's absolutely amazing." She smiled warmly.

"Thank you. "

Later, as the night wore on and Simon had drifted off somewhere, I got a chance to talk to Laura on her own.

"Hey, the last time I saw you was after that awful

accident," I reminded her.

"Indeed. What a day."

"How were you after it? How were the kids?"

She sighed. "Well, I was pretty shaken up. But it was more the shock and the realisation that it could have been a lot worse."

I nodded.

"But you know what kids are like," she continued. "They're so resilient. A bit of pizza and ice-cream afterwards and they were absolutely fine."

I gave a small chuckle. "Aw, if only everything was always that easy."

"I know! "

Then she paused and viewed me with interest. "What about you?" she asked. "Have you ever wanted kids?"

"Oh, I don't know," I sighed. "I used to think I wanted that – you know, the marriage, the 2.4 kids, the picket fence. But I wonder is that because that's what society expects you to have rather than me actually wanting it. In all honesty I've never really felt broody."

Laura shrugged. "Well it's not for everyone," she agreed. "And anyway, you're doing so well in your career."

"Well, thanks," I said, accepting the compliment. "To be honest," I went on, "I'm sure it's even tougher being a mum."

She nodded and took another sip of her wine. "It can be," she agreed. "It's just the fact that it's non-stop, you know? There's never any time off." She was getting rightly on by this stage. I don't know how many glasses of wine she had knocked back but she was obviously taking full advantage of the free drink. Good for her, I thought. She' s right to enjoy a night off.

"You know what?" she said, the alcohol removing any of her inhibitions and giving her a tipsy, woozy glow. "I felt a bit jealous of you at times."

I let out an incredulous cry. "Of me? Why?"

"Oh, you know," she began, waving her glass slowly around. "Working alongside my husband day in, day out. You probably get to spend more time with him than I do. You probably have lots of banter and fun." She takes another sip. "And then by the time he comes home to me, he's too knackered to do anything. It's dinner, bath, bed, that's it."

I leant my head in my hand and viewed her with interest. "That's funny," I said. "Because I've felt jealous of you at times too."

"Of me? But that's ridiculous! Why?"

"Because you're happily married," I stated. "You have beautiful kids. Simon adores you. He keeps a photo of you and the kids on his desk. He raves about you. Whereas me, well, it seems like I'm just eternally single."

We looked at each other with interest, a hazy, tipsy glow allowing us to be so open and frank with each other.

"Simon raves about me?" she repeated, her voice incredulous.

"Yep. All the time. And he feels guilty when he has to work late. And he wishes he could spend more time at home."

"Well actually," Laura announced, in her slurry tipsy voice, "he's planning to go part-time!"

"Well that's great! He needs a bit of a break!"

"Yep! He's gonna go part-time and I'm going to go back to hairdressing part-time – and then we'll split our time at home looking after the kids!"

"Aw, that's amazing, Laura! That'll be such a nice change for you."

"It really will!" she slurred. "I'll be able to leave the house and talk to adults every day!"

I laughed.

"And hey!" she said. "If you ever want your hair done, you can phone me up. I'll give you a huge discount!"

"You're on!"

She pointed a slurry finger at me and observed, "You strike me as someone who prefers to be single ."

"Hmm," I mused. "Maybe you're right."

"And," she continued, "may I inform you that marriage really isn't all it's cracked up to be."

"It isn't?"

She waved a hand away. "Oh you know what we're like. The grass is always greener on the other side."

At that point an inebriated Barry returned to our table and tried to muscle in on our conversation.

"Nice one, Ker," he slurred, placing a heavy drunken arm around my shoulders. "Winning that award. You're going places, Miss."

"Thanks Barry," I squirmed. He was a good sort really. I'd never had any problems working with him, but a drunken Barry slung around your shoulder and leering over you was not such a delightful prospect.

Laura raised an interested eyebrow, watching the scene unfold before her.

"Whad'you think, Laura?" Barry asked. "If me and Kerry get together, we could be a power couple eh?"

Laura's face broke into a smirk and she winked in my direction. "Oh I don't know Barry," she joked.

"Barry," I purred, trying to get rid of him. "If you really want to charm us two ladies, perhaps you could go up and get us another two glasses of wine?"

"I'm on it!" he said, standing up with a swagger. And he was off on an expedition.

"You see?" Laura said, her face in a mischievous grin. "You're really not interested."

We were both giggling when Simon returned to the table. His face lit up when he saw our camaraderie.

"You two look like you're having fun!" he announced.

"Yeah we are," we both said.

"And Laura's offered to do my hair."

"Jeez, you're brave," he joked.

"Oy you!" Laura said, draping an arm around him.

Simon smiled. "So have you told Kerry my news?" he asked.

"I might have hinted at it," Laura said, unsure if she was allowed to spill the beans.

"Going part-time," he announced. "I can't wait. There'll be lie-ins and I'll be relaxing and reading the paper. Hey, Ker, they'll be looking for someone to fill my boots when I leave." He winked, as though I'd be interested in taking on his post.

"Yeah right, Simon. I think it's gonna take me some time to climb that part of the ladder, don't you?"

"You'll do it," Simon said, assuredly.

"Yeah, you will," Laura agreed.

Simon turns to Laura and asked, "Can we go home now? I'm knackered."

"Okay Grandad, let's get you home to bed," Laura jokes.

"Grandad!" Simon mimics. "Bloody cheek! I suppose that means I'm not getting a shag tonight then?"

"We'll see," Laura jokes. "If you play your cards right, you might."

Then she turns to give me a hug and proffers her phone number in my hand. "Here's my number – phone anytime about the hair appointment yeah? It's been so lovely chatting to you. And congrats again. You really deserve it."

Chapter Thirty-Six

<u>Kate</u>

"Welcome everyone. Welcome to the book launch of my very dear friend, Guy Morgan. His book, What Lies Beneath, is hitting the number one spots in many bookshops throughout the country. Guy, we're delighted to have you here tonight. Is there anything you'd like to say to your audience?"

I watch as Guy steps towards the platform and listen as the ripple of applause and cheer spreads throughout the room.

"Thank you, thank you," Guy smiles as he confidently talks into the microphone. "I'm so grateful that you have all come along tonight, I really am."

The host, local celebrity and television presenter, Bee Sands, grins broadly at him. "Now tell us, Guy, what exactly prompted you to write about a young woman trapped in the basement? Where did you find your inspiration for the story?"

She waits expectantly as Guy leans in towards the microphone to give his answer.

"Well, Bee," he says, with a cheeky grin on his face, "I can guarantee you, it's not from personal experience. I most certainly did not have a woman trapped in my basement for research purposes." He looks over at me and winks. "I don't think my girlfriend would have been too understanding if I had told her that one."

A ripple of laughter spreads out among the room and I grin back at him, giving him a knowing wink.

Bee laughs. "Indeed not!" she says. "I'm sure it was all just from imagination!"

Bee continues with some further questions, and then an actress is called to the microphone to give a reading of an extract from the book. Everyone listens in attentive silence, before a three-piece band sing some catchy fifties tunes. Prosecco is poured, a party commences and people get to their feet to dance.

Hannah is there. It's her first night out and I'm keeping a close eye on her. I told her that at any point in the evening she wishes to go home, she only needs to give me the nod and we'd be off. I watch as she's hitting the dance floor, a glass of Prosecco making her relaxed enough to not care about Kyle.

Anyway, ever since Kerry's wonderful work of interrogating him and getting the truth out of him, the case went extremely well. Kyle broke down in court and confessed everything. Not only was Hannah's solicitor fantastically gifted at cross-examining him, but the recordings of his confessions to Kerry meant that they had rock-solid evidence against him. Kyle didn't have a hope in hell. Apparently Kerry had even won an award at her police station for her wonderful interrogation skills. I think she was even given a promotion.

In court, Hannah and Julia had looked on in stunned silence as Kyle was sentenced to seven years in prison. He was given the possibility of parole after three and half years. His crime? Malicious attack towards Hannah causing the loss of her baby and malicious attack and rape of Julia.

Everyone thought he should have got longer of course, but we were at least grateful to see him behind bars. At least Hannah and Julia would be able to sleep in their beds at night now.

Hannah meanwhile had decided to move back into the basement. Even though Kyle was locked up, she still said she preferred it down there. I think it's the first time she'd felt safe and she has a bit of a connection with it. Bless her. I think it's just going to take time – a lot of time – to recover. When Guy signed his publishing deal, he asked Hannah if she would work for him – paid of course – as his PA and typist. She readily agreed even though she didn't want to take any money off him but he wouldn't hear of it. He set up a makeshift office in the basement for her and she sits at the computer typing up his chapters and drinking coffee. She says she loves it. She also meets up with Julia once in a while for coffee and they occasionally attend a support group. She goes to counselling and spends a lot of time doing creative craft classes. I know it's going to take her a long time but she's well on her way to recovery, and we're more than happy to be alongside her every step of the way.

Guy makes a bee-line towards me when he has finally finished signing all his books.

"Well hello you, published author," I smile at him as he bounds over.

"Hey!" he grins. "Oh my goodness, Kate. This is just the best night ever!"

I give him a huge hug. "You so deserve it Guy, you really do. I'm so proud of you."

He grins back. "Well it's all thanks to you, Kate. If you hadn't been so understanding about it all then…"

"Ahh shush," I say, humbly. "You're the one who put all the hard work in."

A press photographer passes at that moment. "Hey, Guy, can I get a few photos?"

"Ah, sure!" he says.

The photographer looks at me. "Are you the writer's girlfriend?"

I smile proudly. "I am indeed!"

It's funny. Usually when Guy and I have been at work events, it's usually on my territory. People are usually asking him, "Are you Kate's partner?" I know that bothered him. I know that the fact that he was working at home as a writer and I was the main breadwinner, made him feel less than. I'm delighted for him that the tables are turning, that the photographer's question has highlighted this to him.

"I am his very proud girlfriend!" I announce, lacing my arm through his and smiling broadly at him.

He grins back and the photographer picks that precise moment to press the button. It is the image that is used the next day for the newspaper headline.

Local writer hits the bestseller list.

And another paper uses his headline for their story.

Double-whammy celebration for local author.

"Guy," I say, my voice more earnest as I look at him intently. "You know the way we had that conversation a while ago about the marriage thing?"

"Hmm?" he says, his concentration not entirely with me, his head still buzzing with all the noise and partying around him.

"Well I've been thinking about it a lot, ever since the stuff that's happened with Hannah, and it's really made me think, you know, it's made me think that I'm ready." I root around in my pocket and pull out a small box.

"Guy," I begin. "It's usually the man who asks this question, but we all know what happened the last time you tried to do that, and I could kick myself for it." I smile awkwardly, a lump forming in my throat. "So this time," I continue, "I'm going to bite the bullet and I'm going to do the asking."

I proffer the box in his direction.

"Guy Morgan, will you make me the happiest girl in the world and be my husband?"

I watch, tears springing to my eyes as I see the look of shock appear over his face. I watch as his hands open the small box, as they see the most beautiful engagement ring in the world that I have picked for myself. And then I watch as a smile spreads over his face, leading into a full sized grin.

"Kate Peters, you surprise me every day. Only you could want to pick your own engagement ring and propose when it suits you. And I love you for it. You're strong, you're independent, and you know what you want. And you want me!" He laughs, pulls me into a hug and kisses me. "So is that a yes then?"

He nods vigorously. "Yes, it's a yes! It was a yes years ago!"

I laugh and then we kiss. And by that stage people around us have started to figure out what is going on and more cheers erupt.

Chapter Thirty-Seven

<u>Hannah</u>

My eyes slowly adjust to my bearings as I gradually awake. I can feel him curled into the nook of my arm, his heat radiating towards me. I look down at him, his dark eyes staring up at me as he stretches. I reach down and place my fingers on his belly, lightly tickling. He purrs in appreciation. It's Furry, my cat companion. It was Guy and Kate who suggested it might be a good idea for me to get a furry friend. I traipsed off to the local rescue centre and picked the cat that looked most terrified, most vulnerable. The first few nights I had him, he slept in the corner of the room under my desk. But gradually, in time, he has worked his way from the cramped corner to a sprawling position in the middle of my bed.

I get up and pad towards the sink, getting a fresh bowl of water for Furry and a glass of sparkling water for me.

The early morning sunlight is peeking through the small window at the top of the room. Even after several attempts to live in Guy and Kate's spare room, we came to an arrangement where I can still be in their basement flat. It sounds silly, but I'm not ready to move out yet. I feel safe here. Even though Kyle is locked up, I still crave the safety of living cocooned in this little haven. Maybe it's the fact that Guy and Kate are living upstairs and I feel their protective boundary around me, I don't know. But we came to an arrangement - I work for Guy, typing up all his chapters and dealing with any of his admin writerly stuff, and I get to live here for free. They also give me money towards food and a bit of pocket money. I'm ever so grateful, I really am. But

Guy insists that he's the one who's grateful. He says he'd never be able to reach his new deadlines if it wasn't for me typing away like a demon in the basement. I don't mind though, I enjoy it. When I'm sitting typing I can block everything else out. It's just head down, and type. I don't think of anything else.

I don't think about the court case and the way that Kyle stared at me with such disgust from across the court room. I don't think about the way his solicitor cross-examined me, asking me so many horrible questions about my drinking. And I don't think about the look on his face when he was convicted and sentenced, about the way that he was led down to the dock with his hands in cuffs.

I should have been happy, of course I should. But I felt nothing. No, that's not true. I felt a mixture of things – guilt, relief, numbness, shock. I wanted to feel like it was my happy ending – that Kyle had had his comeuppance and the rest of his years would be locked behind bars, with his days dragging. But part of me couldn't quite believe it. How long would he actually be behind bars? What if his sentence was massively reduced for good behaviour? What about the day that he was released? Would he come after me? What would he do to me then?

There were so many nights that I woke up in a cold sweat after having vivid nightmares. In the nightmare, Kyle had somehow escaped from prison, had come straight to Guy's house, sneaked inside, crept down to the basement and found me. In my nightmare he made a bee-line for my bed, put his hand around my throat and began to choke me. Just as he was choking me, I'd wake up panting and covered in sweat.

I knew that I could text Guy or Kate if I wanted to, that they'd come running downstairs and sit with me. But I didn't want to wake them. And anyway, even knowing that they were upstairs was enough comfort.

"Another nightmare?" Guy asked, as I arrived up the next morning to join him for coffee. He took one look at me and knew from my face that it had been a restless night.

"Yeah, 'fraid so," I replied.

"You know you can phone me. I keep my phone switched on especially."

"I know you do," I sighed. "But it was okay. I just cuddled Furry."

Guy nodded. "Maybe try to get a nap at some stage today, yeah?"

"Yeah," It's funny, when I think of that time I had the mild attraction for Guy, when I used to distract myself from unpleasant sexual acts from Kyle by thinking about Guy, what was that about? It's absolutely gone now. There's no physical attraction at all, instead, an extremely good friendship. He's like a big brother to me, a protective force. I wonder if the attraction at the time was just some sort of distraction technique – a fantasy, a way of escaping my reality.

"It's like you're my knight in shining armour," I joked to him, but he shook his head humbly and said, "Uh-huh, you're your own knight. You did it yourself, Hannah. You're the one who had the courage to leave him. All I did was to supply the room."

I shrugged my shoulders, wishing that I could accept the compliment, but things just didn't feel 'fixed' yet. When would I have that feeling of contentment? When would I feel that I could completely relax and never worry about him returning back into my life?

The counsellor said it was some form of PTSD, that it would take time for me to fully recover from the ordeal. I had arranged Skype sessions with her. I was still at that stage where I didn't even want to leave the house. Some sort of irrational fear of bumping into Kyle plagued me. As long as I was cocooned in my basement haven I felt okay. So I chatted with Angela once a week on Skype and she kept an eye on me, often giving me encouraging feedback like, "You are improving. Honestly, I can see it in you even if you can't see it in yourself."

I wanted to believe her but I couldn't. It was as if I was trekking through one murky day after the other, unable to see the light at the end of the tunnel.

Julia kept in touch by Skype too. She suggested that we get out more, but I didn't feel ready. I was quite happy to live as a bit of a hermit. As long as there was no drama then there was no risk of any trouble. A quiet life, that's all I wanted.

Besides, we had one night out and it was enough for me. It was the launch night for Guy's book. I got dressed up. I wore a short skirt and a low-cut top. I only wore it as a sort of "F**k you" to Kyle. After all those times he'd told me off for the way I dressed, I thought it was about time I dressed any way I wanted to. So I layered on a shedload of make-up, tarted myself up and danced with Julia on the dancefloor. There was some interest from a couple of guys that night. But one of them was clearly just after a one-night stand. The other turned out to be a journalist who wanted an inside story for his tacky magazine.

I couldn't wait to get home again, to kick off my high heels, pull on my pyjamas and wipe off my make-up.

And when I arrived home, I switched on the computer to watch a bit of catch-up TV and unwind. I checked my emails and noticed one with the subject header:

Kyle and Hannah forever.

My heart jumped into my mouth and I froze. My fingertips went icy cold as I felt a dread sweep over my entire body. My finger trembled as I clicked on 'open message'.

And there, in the body of the message was a simple:

Kyle and Hannah forever. Promise rings for sale. For a love that will last forever.

I called out for Kate and Guy to come down. I really didn't want to put a dampener on their evening but if I didn't talk to them about it, I'd never sleep.

They both rushed down and examined the email.

"No, don't worry," Guy said with authority. "That's some sort of weird random junk mail."

Kate nodded. "Yeah, it's crazy the way these things work. Honestly, it's nothing to worry about. Look at the email address – it's a random set of squiggly letters. It means nothing."

"Okay," I said even though my mind was still spinning

218

with fear and worry.

Kate gave me a huge hug. "I'm gonna sit down here for a while with you. Let's have some hot chocolate and marshmallows."

"No," I insisted. "I'm okay."

"Hush," she interrupted me. "I want hot chocolate." She turned to Guy. "Stick the kettle on honey, will you?"

"Of course," he agreed, heading towards the sink.

And so we sat, cross-legged, drinking hot chocolate, chatting, petting Furry, until somehow I must have fallen asleep, and they placed a blanket over me and tucked me in.

THE END

Fantastic Books
Great Authors

darkstroke is
an imprint of
Crooked Cat Books

- Gripping Thrillers
- Cosy Mysteries
- Amazing Horrors
- Fascinating Historicals
- Exciting Fantasy
- Young Adult and Children's Adventures
- Non-Fiction

Discover us online
www.darkstroke.com

Find us on instagram:
www.instagram.com/darkstrokebooks

Printed in Poland
by Amazon Fulfillment
Poland Sp. z o.o., Wrocław

60089034R00134